Jackson McIntire moves to a Native American Reservation to become their new school administrator. He will learn much about his new home and the people that live there. Almost immediately, Jackson discovers that his contact person is a very handsome young Lakota chief named Chief John Two Hawks. As his love of the community and its people grow, so does the love he's found in John Two Hawks.

Little Spirit
Copyright © 2023 James J Gregoryk
ISBN: 978-1-4874-3673-5
Cover art by Martine Jardin

Published by eXtasy Books Inc

Look for us online at:
www.eXtasybooks.com

Little Spirit

By

James J Gregoryk

Dedication

Dedicated to Gerald West, Devin, Annika, and to Metka H. Hansen for their love and support. They all believed in me.

CHAPTER ONE

D r. Jackson McIntire arrived at the Native American Independent Nation of the Black Mountain Lakota reservation at 8:00 AM. He'd been hired to be the new school administrator. He stopped at the entrance, got out of his car, and marveled at a giant hand-carved sign with the reservation's name and a message that read, *Welcome to all that come in peace.* On one side of the entry was a magnificent totem pole with carved eagles, bears, mountain lions, and bison sitting on top of the other, looking like they were protecting this place. Jack took pictures of both to send to his family.

He hopped back into his car and drove, bouncing in his seat with excitement. Jack stopped at a building that had a sign that said *Native American Independent Nation of the Black Mountain Lakota Central Administration Office.* He saw an *OPEN* sign hanging on the door. He smiled — that meant he wouldn't have to wait.

He gathered up his proper identification papers, his signed contract, and the housing paperwork. He was given a 4-bedroom house, rent-free, as part of his employee benefits. With everything in hand, he got out of his car, flew up the stairs, and rushed through the door. He was ready to start his new job and see his new home.

Jack could barely stay still long enough to talk to the lady who sat at the front desk. "I'm Dr. Jackson McIntire. I have a meeting with Mr. John Two Hawks."

She watched him and chuckled, but before she could respond to anything, a heavy-set Native American man came out of the back.

Jack quietly asked her, "John Two Hawks?"

She just frowned and quickly shook her head no. She opened her mouth to say something, but the man interrupted her. The guy snapped at Jack, "*Táku yačhíŋ he Itháŋčhaŋ kici John Núŋp Čhetáŋ?*"

Jack looked at the man and stated, "I'm sorry, I don't understand or speak Lakota."

"What do you want with John Two Hawks?"

Jack, in his most professional manner, explained, "I've just arrived, and I have an appointment with Mr. Two Hawks. I'm the new school administrator."

The guy frowned and looked Jack up and down, then crossed his arms. "Get in your car and follow me."

Jack went from smiling to surprised. The lady at the desk rolled her eyes at the man and said something in Lakota. The man answered her and grinned. She frowned and quickly picked up the phone.

Jack complied, as he saw no reason not to follow in his car. They drove a couple of blocks, then stopped at some rundown shack. They walked up to the hut, and this Native American person flung open the rickety door. "Well, Mr. Administrator, this will be your new home."

Jack made a quick scan around the falling down building.

Feeling very confused, Jack said plainly, "I don't think so. This place doesn't meet any of the requirements of my contract." Jack started out the door, and the man grabbed him by the arm and pulled him back.

"You'll take what I say you'll take." The man huffed and shoved Jack's forehead with his index finger.

Jack's temper flared. That guy outweighed Jack by a hundred and fifty pounds. Without a moment's hesitation, Jack laid him out with one move. The man squealed like a hog.

Suddenly, another guy rushed through the door.

Jack glared and shouted at him, "You'll be next!"

The new man, a very handsome Native American, put his hands up as if to say *I surrender* and *calm down* simultaneously. "I'm John Two Hawks. The office secretary, Missy Red Sky, told me I needed to come here. Who are you, and what are you doing in this rattletrap of a building? And why is Hank on the floor with your foot on his face and you yanking his arm off?"

"Big Chief Ass for a Face here thought he could push me around and even put his hands on me. He told me this was my new living quarters."

"Big Chief" — the man laughed his head off, stuttering out his words — "Ass for a Face" — he took a deep breath and belly-laughed again. "I'm going to pee myself. Hank, you'll never live this down! Big Chief Ass for a Face, you're killing me!" The man seemed to gather himself until he looked at the man on the floor again. "Oh God, I'm going to pee myself, I swear." He doubled over with laughter and didn't seem able to get himself together at all. Every time he almost did, he started over again. Finally together, he said, "Sorry, I'm John Two Hawks, and could you get your foot off his face, please? How'd you take Hank out like that?"

Jack released the man and calmed down quickly. "I come from a huge farm family, and I'm the youngest. So I learned to take care of myself."

"Listen, I'm so sorry for his behavior. It will never happen again. Will it, Big Chief Ass for a Face?"

Hank said defensively, "I was giving this little outsider a hard time. How was I to know the little shit had no sense of humor and turned instantly meaner than an angry badger?"

That smart-ass statement made Jack react. He moved toward Hank.

John grabbed him around the waist just in time and said to Hank, "I'd run if I were you, *Chief*, or I just may let him go."

Hank hauled ass, and within seconds, he flew out the door, hopped in his car, and sped off. They watched him leave.

"Let me start this off right," the new man began.

"You're still holding me," Jack said.

John released him. "Oops, I'm sorry. Again, let me start this off right. I'm Chief John Two Hawks, son of Thomas Three Elks, Elder Chief of the Black Mountain Lakota, and Jena Little Flower, his Chief Medical Officer." He leaned in, smiled, and raised his eyebrows. Jack refused to give him a reaction. "That's a joke. She's our medicine woman and a spiritual guide. That jerk you just clobbered was Hank Flying Crow, aka Big Chief Ass for a Face." A short burst of laughter shot out from John. He put his fist to his mouth and feigned a cough. "Sorry, but that still just kills me."

Jack's eyebrows knitted as he glared at John.

"Obviously, not funny to you. You must be Dr. Jackson Lee McIntire. I'm the one you have a scheduled meeting with this morning." He stuck out his hand. "Welcome to The Native American Independent Nation of the Black Mountain Lakota, and please forgive my tribe member, as he thinks he's funny, but in reality, he's an idiot. To be totally upfront, he and several other members weren't in favor of your appointment, but the council approved you, so that's that."

Jack felt his face pale a little. "I really want this job."

"You were the most qualified candidate, which is why you got the job." John offered his hand.

They shook hands, and Jack looked directly into his soft and inviting brown eyes. He gasped at the handsomeness of this man. His dark golden-brown skin and his long raven-black hair shone blue in the sunlight. His hair flowed with every movement. He wore jeans and a white t-shirt, which showed off his muscular body. John looked all male, very masculine—he really was a total stud. His face was perfect, with high cheek bones and a dimpled chin. But his beautiful smile was what captivated Jack.

"*Hello*? Dr. McIntire?" John smiled directly at Jack.

Jack snapped out of it and immediately checked his mouth—he hadn't drooled—then said, "I'm sorry. It's nice to meet you, Chief John Two Hawks, son of Chief Thomas Three Elks and Jena Little Flower. Will that man be back any time soon?"

"No, Dr. McIntire." John looked at the cloud of dust Hank had left. "I don't think that'll happen any time soon. Let's get you to your new home and settled. We have a tribal meeting this afternoon at one. When will your stuff arrive? And do I need to get you any furniture? Also, FYI, I would prefer you didn't use the language I just heard around the children."

Jack shot him an embarrassed look. "I would never. He just..." Jack blushed with embarrassment, but he pulled himself together. "Please, it's Jack. I'd love to get to my new home to clean up and put away some of my stuff. All my furniture arrives tomorrow so I can't tell if I need anything else, yet. Why are you having a meeting in five hours? And am I required to attend all the powwows as part of my contract? Because it wasn't in there, was it?" Jack asked.

Chuckling, John said, "We don't have powwows per se." He put it in finger quotes and smirked. "We mostly have tribal or council meetings." John chuckled as Jack felt his face redden, embarrassed by his outdated words.

John continued, "Yes and no about attending meetings. I'd like you always to attend, but it's not a part of your contract, but it's a part of being involved in the community."

Jack, still flushed, awkwardly replied, "I'm so sorry, I'm not a total idiot, just not educated about what's the right and wrong terminology and which is the correct thing to say or do, but I'll learn."

John stared at him with a puzzled expression. Then his gaze widened with understanding. "Ah, yeah, whatever. Oh, that!" John politely waved him off. "We're used to it. Television and low-budget movies screwed things up about what we're called, what we do, and who we are. Just listen carefully and be observant. I'm quite sure you'll catch on quickly." He smiled at Jack, and Jack's knees went weak and he sort of stumbled for a second.

John instantly took his arm, preventing from falling.

That man and his wonderful smile proved to be a hard thing for Jack to ignore. "I'm fine. Thanks for your help." Jack smiled back, and their gazes locked momentarily.

Chapter Two

John led the way out of the shack. He glanced in the direction Hank had taken off and shook his head. "Big Chief Ass for a Face. That kills me." He looked at Jack and smiled. "You know, for a little dude, you're quite the tough guy." Jack smiled at the compliment, then blushed as John added with his hands in the air, "Sorry if I've offended you. I don't want your foot in my face." John's playful smile said it all.

Jack froze for a second, then said, "I'm so sorry about the Big Chief Ass for a Face remark. It sounds so racist and stupid. I'll apologize to Hank Flying Crow next time I see him."

John immediately replied, "Oh no, you won't! Hank can be a total jerk sometimes, and putting him in his place showed your strength of character. Hank needs that at times, so you'll let it go."

Jack's smile stretched across his face. "I think we're going to be good friends."

John nodded acknowledgment. "Follow me in your car. Your accommodations are just down the road. I think you'll like what we've done to the place so far."

John hopped into his truck and started it. Immediately, he called his best friend, Screaming Eagle. "Hey, it's me, John. I just met the new school administrator. When I saw a picture of Dr. Jackson Lee McIntire, to be honest, it didn't do much for me, but after I saw him face-to-face, I just can't believe how incredibly handsome he is, well, good-looking, no, really, I think he's gorgeous!" When John told him about Hank's new name, Screaming Eagle laughed so hard that he nearly choked.

John told his friend, "I've never really been attracted to light-skinned people, but Jackson's something to behold. I want to scoop him up and take him home with me."

Screaming Eagle started laughing at John. "Dude, you need to get your shit together and act like a chief and not a drooling idiot. After all we went through to get him, we don't want our new administrator to turn tail and run, now, do we? Did he really out and out flatten Fat Hank?"

"I saw Hank flat on the ground with Dr. McIntire's foot on his face with my own eyes," John said laughingly. "I think Jack would take me out if I even tried something. He seems to take things pretty seriously."

Screaming Eagle cautioned, "Well, don't be falling totally in love with that little man just yet. You only met a few minutes ago, and you tend to act the fool."

John and Jack had reached Jack's new home, so John said goodbye to Screaming Eagle and hung up. They both got out of their cars and walked to the door. John caught Jack giving him the eye several times.

Every time John looked at Jack, he saw something more attractive about him. He hoped Jack didn't notice, or he might think he was a total perv. Jack never indicated that he noticed anything or that John was practically drooling over him. John paid so much attention to the sound of Jack's voice and watched Jack so intently that he tripped over his own feet twice.

Jack glanced to the side and smiled at him. "Maybe I should be quiet. You don't seem to be able to listen and walk at the same time."

John embarrassingly replied, "I can, too!" Falling slightly behind Jack, John slapped his forehead with an *I-am-an-absolute-dweeb* forehead slap. "Now I look and sound like a stupid drooling freak," he said, not so quietly.

Jack smirked and replied, "Don't we all have those moments?"

John murmured, "God, I just can't get enough of him."

Jack queried, "Excuse me? I'm not sure what you said."

"Oh, God, it was nothing, just talking to myself," John feebly answered. He stepped forward, unlocked, and opened the door to Jack's new home.

Jack smiled. "Do you do that a lot, and always out loud?" Jack smiled even more broadly as he entered his new home.

His expression alone gave John every indication that their renovations on the house had turned it into the perfect home for their new school administrator.

Native American objects hung all over the place. "I love all the beautiful artifacts." Jack turned around in awe and told John, "I'm blown away by my new house. It's just so . . . wow!" Saying the same thing several more times made John smile wider every time. Jack wandered around the house. The living room contained a magnificent stone fireplace with a giant moose head that hung above it. He whispered, "Note to self, take down the dead animal, yuck." The hardwood floors and wooden cabinets made the house truly a home that others only dreamed about.

John showed him through the entire house and explained the history. His great-aunt had owned the home, and she'd left it to the tribe to be the housing for the head administrator of the school.

He looked at Jack. "I'll have someone come up and take down the moose head, I never thought it was a great idea, but Hank . . . never mind, it comes down."

Jack just stood and stared at John. Finally he said, "I can't tell you how wonderful I find my new home."

John smiled. "That's such a good thing."

They sat and chatted for a little while. John asked Jack to tell him about himself. Jack filled him in on some family stuff—that he came from a very large family and was the youngest. But mostly, he talked about how excited he was about his new job.

John welcomed him once again and suggested that they exchange cell numbers so they could call each other when they needed information. Then John helped him take everything from the car and put it in the house. They sat on the front porch for a few more minutes and talked about Jack's duties and responsibilities. John also told him about growing up on the reservation. He, too, came from a fairly large family.

John stood and brushed off his pants. "I've got to run, but I'll see you at the powwow later." John finger quoted and chuckled. "By the way, if you get a chance to run over to the school, my sister, Donna Yellow Bird's the office manager and your secretary. I told her you'd stop by today. I think you'll really like her."

Jack stood and held out his hand. John took it and shook it gently, but held on for longer than he needed. Finally, he smiled and let go. "Later." He left Jack to get settled in.

John met up with Screaming Eagle, and for a couple of hours, they worked on some tribal issues. John talked non-stop about Jackson and how he'd see him again at the powwow. Jack's choice of words had both of them chuckling. Jack's innocence about their culture made for an amusing time.

John talked about how Jack came across as so genuine and that he'd never seen a more beautiful human being.

Screaming Eagle raised one eyebrow and said, "Without a doubt, you're in such trouble. You need to be thinking with your big head, not your little one."

John smiled, then frowned. "I'll just have to be careful not to be clingy or too pushy, but Dr. Jackson Lee McIntire just might be the one for me."

Screaming Eagle stared at John and cleared his throat. "Yeah, just be careful and don't pant or drool on him." He noticed a fairly large wet spot on John's pants. "Dude, you really need to get control of yourself. You're leaking or something. You have a major wet spot on your pants. I think I'm going to gag."

John turned beet red, covered the area, then readjusted his junk. "Why were you even checking that out? Man, that's just so weird."

It was Screaming Eagle who blushed this time.

Jack picked up his notebook and hurried off to see the school. On the way, he saw a wolf or some big dog, and it seemed like it followed him. He shrugged it off as being just a dog, maybe a shepherd or husky. Jack's walk to the school only took eight minutes.

Jack stopped and slowly entered the school building. Right away, he saw things that needed attention—some peeling paint in the entry way, floors needing to be stripped and re-finished, and even a cracked window. He duly noted it all in his notebook to discuss with John when he next saw him.

Jack glanced over toward what he assumed was the school office. He then noticed a woman sitting at a desk. She spotted him at the same time and smiled broadly.

She hurried out of the office to introduce herself. "*Taŋyáŋ yahí*. Welcome. I'm Donna Yellow Bird, John's sister and your secretary. John said you'd probably be coming over here." Donna's round, short body bounced as she approached Jack with her hand stretched to him. Her eyes sparkled, and her smile matched John's.

"Hello, yes, John told me about you, too. I'm Jackson McIn-tire, the new school administrator." They shook hands, and she squeezed his hand with great affection. Then quite unexpectedly, she pulled Jack into a full-blown body hug.

Jack smiled, and he hugged her back.

"I know. John told me all about you and showed me your picture. I love your beautiful green eyes. I hope that we're going to be great friends," Donna said as she stepped back. Her soft-spoken voice sounded melodic and kind. "Let's have a tour of the school."

Donna took his arm, and they started walking. First was his office. It was small but worked for him. Then they moved through the school in general, where he noticed the library desperately needed books, and he quickly added that to his list. As they traveled through the school, Jack observed that, overall, the school appeared neat and clean.

Donna stopped and listened for a second. "I've got to go and answer the phone. I'll meet up with you in a few minutes. The cafeteria and elementary grades are to your left, and computer labs, gym, and high school are to your right." She left him to wander around on his own and headed back to the office.

Walking down the hallways, Jack noted that animal heads hung on the walls and that they should probably come down. But he would find out more about them when he talked with John. When he walked into the restroom, it looked okay, but when he tried to open the stall doors, all of them were locked. He simply used his pocketknife and popped open the first one. No toilet, just a hole with some rags stuffed in it, none in the second or third or fourth. He scurried around the entire school, checking all the restrooms. He found only three working toilets in the whole school and in the boy's restrooms, no urinals at all.

Donna returned and met him in the hall. "Donna, I'm confused. In just a little over two weeks, nearly three hundred children will start school. Equally important is the fact that in about three days, we'll have our first Departments of

Education inspection with no functional restrooms. Donna, what on earth's going on here? I found only three working toilets in the entire building. Have the toilets and urinals already been scheduled for installation?" Jack watched as Donna made a face. "Donna, I don't like that face you're giving me. How about, are they scheduled for delivery, so everything can be installed?" Again, she gave him the look of anguish. Jack asked, "What?"

She finally said very sadly and meekly, "You'll have to talk to Hank Flying Crow, although I've heard from my brother that you renamed him Chief Ass for a Face, which is a much better fit." Her laughter floated down the hallways. One look at Jack's angry face and Donna regained her composure. "Come with me. There's so much more you need to check out, like the computer labs." She led him to Computer Lab I. When she opened the door, his mouth dropped, and he stood staring. Jack's mouth moved like he was searching for words but couldn't find them. There sat only one very, very, old and probably non-functioning computer in a room meant for twenty-five.

Jack looked absolutely dumbfounded. "What on earth's happening here? Part of our educational contract was that two new labs would be set up and ready for student use. The Departments of Education gave us a bunch of computers for the school as part of a grant. They'd expect to see them up and running during their inspection." Jack's eyebrows furrowed, and his expression became harsh. "Donna, I hate confusion. Everyone has to know about the scheduled inspection and that the people from the state departments from two districts are coming specifically to inspect the entire set-up. These people will want to ensure the new instruction programs are up and running. All of which were paid for with the grants we got for the school through these departments of education. They're coming to see that the programs, specifically designed for this school to use, are properly installed and implemented. Everyone here has to know this, right?" Jack again asked Donna, "Is there a mistake? Have the computers not arrived?"

She sounded sad as she quietly responded, "What everyone thinks they know and what's real are two different things. I've tried to get them to listen, but no one has, so you'll have to ask Chief Ass for a Face."

No laughter came from Jack. He found no humor in the fact that the school wasn't in workable shape. He tore off his list of things to do and gave it to Donna. "Most of the stuff on the list is routine maintenance, but not the restrooms or labs." He instructed her to please call whoever she needed to, so those things got done.

Jack marched back toward his new house. He called his dad and vented. "I spent hours and hours being trained to implement the special program. Native Americans from here designed this entire program for Native American children, and boards made the school its test case. It seems I'm the only one who understands the importance of the whole situation."

His father only said, "Let them explain before you go off to crazy town."

Jack said his goodbyes and hung up. He continued toward his house.

Jack noticed that something moved, and he got a glimpse of that weird dog again, and he told the dog, "Please stop following me. I've enough to worry about."

He tried to call John as he rushed to the house, but no answer. He walked inside the house and seriously considered packing his stuff up again. His cellphone rang, and he looked and saw John's name. "Hello."

John asked, "Did you forget the council meeting?"

Jack replied, "I'm on my way." He hung up. Jack then noticed that someone had removed the moose head. He debated, then quickly wrote out his resignation, just in case he needed to back out of this situation. Jack headed out the door to the Council Hall.

His brother called as he walked to the hall. Jack informed him about the situation. "I'm on my way to a meeting. I need answers to what's happening here."

Like their father, Jason warned, "Take caution, and for God's sake, listen."

The Council Hall was a colossal round building made of massive timbers, stone, and concrete. It looked old, yet very well taken care of. As he arrived, the large set of double doors stood open for him. He entered the building. Inside, Jack saw the semi-circular table. It looked as though these people were in charge. Jack froze for a second when he saw their solemn expressions.

He took in a deep breath and marched right up to the center person, an older man, who sat slightly separated from the rest. Jack handed him his written resignation and said, "You must be the head man here, so I guess I need to hand you my resignation. It seems that much of what was promised won't happen. The school isn't nearly ready for any kind of inspection."

As he turned to walk back out, he saw John and that older man beside him standing. "You'll not leave, Little Spirit," the older man said and sat back down. The big doors closed, and two guys stood in front of it.

"What! Am I being held hostage? Where do you people think we are, in some western movie or something?" He looked to John. John's smile was gone, and he looked angry. Jack turned to directly face John. "You lied to me about the school."

John blushed. "I know it needs a little more painting and stuff, and we're working on that, I promise. However, we've kept it very clean and fully equipped."

Jack took a step back. He felt even more confused. "There's some confusion here. The school isn't fully equipped. For example, there are three working toilets in the entire school building. Three hundred-plus kids and twenty-two-plus adults will be attending this school. Not only is that illegal, but it's absolutely not functional, not to mention the sanitary issues. The library looks to have about half of the books needed for a school this size. There were to be two completely functional, fully equipped, computer labs so we can implement the program you all agreed to use. They should be set up and running by now. You signed a contract! A contract that I negotiated between two different departments of education. They gave you ninety computers, seventy for the labs, fifteen for the library, and five for the staff. There's only one old, useless computer in one lab and zero in the other."

The shocked expression on everyone's faces surprised Jack. He began to understand what Donna meant when she said, *"What everyone thinks they know and what is real are two different things."* The looks alone made him understand that what this group of people believed and what the real condition of things were in conflict. Jack continued, "Donna told me I had to talk with Chief . . . sorry, Hank Flying Crow, so I could get an explanation. Why would that be?"

All eyes focused on Hank, who clumsily tried to stand. "Now, now, now let me explain. I can sell them computers for a great deal of money, and we can use some money for the American-Canadian Buffalo Hunt Celebration that's coming up this fall and even more important, to buy things that the entire community can profit from . . . and come on, how many toilets do a few kids need anyway?"

John's personality completely changed. He no longer held that calm demeanor Jack had experienced. John stood up and leaped over the table. He moved instantly to Hank, almost as if he'd flown there. John leaned in with hands on the table so they were face-to-face. "Listen carefully to me, we're going to be audited, and we'll be observed and evaluated, and if we don't live up to the expectations of the boards of education, both the US and Canadian board and their inspection committees, they'll shut us down. We'll have let down all of our people that developed the course of study for our children, and we'll lose our school! Those computers and this man are our only hope of keeping our school open. More importantly, we'll have let down our children."

John stepped back. "I don't want our children educated in the schools off the reservation, do you? Without all the equipment and the upgrade in the restrooms and the cleanup of the rest of the building, plus the upgrade of materials in the library, we're going to have to close the school. Which means we'll have to pay back those departments of education nearly a million dollars. We signed a contract. You've totally failed the school, the children, and our nation! You need to be banned from this council, the community, and from the reservation!" John turned back to Jack and the council. "Can we still fix this?"

"Maybe, if we get everything done." Jack looked back at the council. They all stood, and their expressions had changed. They no longer looked solemn. They looked angry.

John looked at Jack. "When are the people from the departments of education coming?"

"Monday morning, and we can't reschedule," Jack said.

A verbal explosion occurred. The entire council's anger hit the roof. The building shook.

Jack watched as each member spoke about the situation. Everything was directed at Hank. Finally, the center chief raised his hand, and the room was instantly silenced. He looked directly at Hank. "We've only until Monday morning before the inspectors arrive to have everything up and running at our school. It's all on you. *No* argument. *No* discussion.

We must have this done regardless of what it takes."

He turned to Jack and said, "Dr. McIntire, I'm Thomas Three Elks, Elder Chief of this Lakota Nation. Will you stay and let us make this right? Please. It took much spirit of the soul to stand before us. You're a little man with a big spirit. Stay with us, Little Spirit, and help us with our school."

The powerful man looked so sincere as he pleaded for him to please stay. Jack nodded his head yes, then bowed when his tears started to well up. Jack tried so hard not to let the tears flow in front of these powerful men. Having been so humbled by this man, it was impossible to stop his tears, no matter what he did.

Two gentle arms encircled him and pulled him in close. "You cry, Little Spirit, you've proved you've the soul of the hawk and the heart of a warrior. You showed great bravery to stand your ground and state your case to the council," John said as he held Jack in his arms.

Jack heard no sounds. When he recovered enough, he stepped back to thank Chief Thomas Two Elks and the council, but everyone had disappeared, all of them, like the wind had taken them away.

"I need to say thank you to them all," Jack said as he looked around and searched for everyone.

John smiled at him. "You did, Little Spirit, with your tears. I'll take you home now."

As the two of them started to leave, John saw a strange look come over Jack. He turned very pale, and his speech sounded confused. Then he started to crumble. Jack's eyes rolled back, his head tilted back, and his knees suddenly gave out. John caught him up before he hit the ground. He shuffled Jackson in his arms and hurried out the doors. Something was terribly wrong. John shouted for help as soon as he shot through the doors. His mother came on a dead run and ushered him with Little Spirit draped in his arms into John's house. He frantically told his mother what had just happened.

Jack woke up and looked around, unsure what had just happened, but he found himself in a strange bed, and to his surprise, a wolf with golden eyes sat staring at him. "That's a real live wolf sitting here," Jack said aloud. "I must be dreaming some strange dream."

Waking up, more reality hit him. He froze and stared at the wolf. Jack noticed several strangers staring at him. "Wolf!" Jack managed to squeak out.

A woman said, "Get on out of here, Bambi, you're scaring that boy!" She turned and gently spoke to Jack. "Do you know where you are?"

Jack shook his head. "No, I don't have a wolf, and I don't have a bed in my house yet."

The people in the room collectively chuckled. Jack realized there were other women standing in the room, too. The first woman spoke again, "Dr. Winters's been called, it seems you passed out, and John brought you here to his house. I've never seen him in such a state before." The other women standing in the room nodded in agreement.

Jack asked, "Could you please tell me who you are and why was there a wolf hanging around in here glaring at me?"

The woman smiled. "I'm Jena Little Flower, wife of Thomas Two Elks and mother of John. These are my younger twin sisters, May and Mary. We're the trained medical staff who care for the sick around these parts. The wolf's John's dog or wolf, whatever you'd call it. Can I please call John in here before he drives us all crazy?"

Jack looked at her suspiciously, but then he nodded. Jena opened the door, and in a blink of an eye, John appeared and knelt beside the bed.

"Are you okay, Little Spirit? You really scared me."

Jack felt puzzled. "I think so. By the way, this Little Spirit thing? Exactly what's that all about?"

John smiled broadly. "The chief of all the Lakota has given you this name. I hope you'll come to see it as a truly great honor."

Intrigued, Jack asked, "He named me? Why? From everything I've read, I thought that never happened outside of the tribe members. I hoped I'd one day get an Indian name, oops, Native American name, but I was thinking maybe Wild Mustang. I'm just babbling, aren't I?"

The ladies all nodded in agreement. Everyone around him chuckled. Now he knew for sure that he'd been babbling.

John raised his eyebrow, and a small burst of laughter followed. "Wild Mustang? Really? That's very funny." But John pulled back his humor.

Looking down at his hand, it shocked Jack that, for some reason, John held his hand. Jack gently pulled it free.

"Little Spirit, you stood up and told us what was going on without fear, and with such spirit, even though you're small in stature, you're going to be one big man to my people, because you showed to the council that our children were more important than all else. The word will spread, and the children will be excited to meet you. You'll be Little Spirit!" Jack met John's gaze, and they were transfixed in each other's eyes for a moment.

"Excuse me, but I hope you aren't giving our patient mouth to mouth resuscitation." With Dr. Winters attempted humor, the sisters all giggled.

Dr. Winters motioned for John to move aside. then checked Jack over. He asked him about his day and what he'd eaten. Jack explained that he'd just plain forgotten about eating with all the excitement.

Dr. Winters told Jena, "I'm sure all of this was caused by the lack of food and excitement. That caused a drop in blood pressure, which caused him to faint. This boy needs to eat and rest." Dr. Winters patted Jack's hand. "Mind Jena, because if you don't, she'll be a force to reckon with." The doctor smiled, gathered his belonging, and left with Jena showing him out.

Jack's phone played his parents' ringtone. Jack said, "Give me that damn phone. Hi, Mom."

"Son, are you okay? Do I need to come there?"

"Nope, I'm fine."

"Jackson, what happened?"

"Yes, I guess I fainted. I just forgot to eat anything today with all the excitement and stuff going on here."

"You've never fainted before, are you sure you are okay? This very nice young man, John Two Hawks, has kept me up to date.

"Yes, he's a very nice man." Jack winked playfully at John.

"Sweetheart, I need to talk with him again."

He looked at his phone totally confused, and said to John, "Here, she wants to talk to you." He handed the phone to John.

"John, please keep me informed about my son. Thanks so much."

"I promise. Bye for now."

John hung up.

"What did she say?" Jack asked.

John quietly responded, "Little Spirit, sometimes there are things you just don't need to know, or you should wait and see how things turn out." John reached down and helped Jack up, then picked him up into his arms.

"What the heck? Put me down, you giant oaf!"

John met his definite glare and said, "You're going to eat. When I'm satisfied you're no longer in danger, you'll go back to bed, and you'll sleep, got it?" John looked serious as he spoke.

Jack bristled. "You can't tell me what I will and won't do. Just who in the hell do you think you are anyway?" Jack saw that wolf again, and this time she showed him all her teeth. Jack pointed at her. "I'm pretty sure she placed me on her menu." He snuggled in closer to John.

"Bambi, you need to go outside," John told the wolf, and she left the room.

John clearly stated, "So you know I've got to call your mom back in thirty minutes, and then I'll tell her if she's needed here or not."

"You wouldn't fucking dare do that!" Jack asked in horror.

"Wanna bet? Just try me."

"Fine, you big cheater, fine, put me down, damn it. I can walk. I think that wolf or dog or whatever, is thinking about eating me. Put me down, please."

John set him down, and Jack stood. It lasted for all of about three seconds. Then the blood rushed from his head, he went pale, and his legs turned all rubbery.

Picking Jack back up into his arms, John said, "Yeah, Mr. I Can Walk. Sure you can! And by the way, that mouth of yours . . . totally filthy. Do you eat with that mouth?" John carried him into the kitchen. He put Jack at the table and pulled a chair beside him like when you fed a child. "Eat!" he commanded.

"I can't possibly eat all of this in a day, let alone at one meal," Jack whined.

He caught the scent of the food, and the wonderful aroma kicked in his appetite, so he started eating.

After one bite, Jack realized that he really needed food.

Jack's eyes rolled back, and he moaned with pleasure. "This food is beyond delicious. What is this?" His mouth filled with delicious, tender meat.

"Barbequed rattlesnake," John said, his eyes twinkling

with mischief.

Jack sprayed food everywhere. He quickly scrubbed his tongue with his napkin and took a huge gulp of water. Jack's eyes teared up.

"Little Spirit, I'm just teasing you. It's range chicken with wild rice and prairie spices."

"I hate snakes!" Jack harshly said, "And you just about gave me a heart attack!"

Whack! The sound of a wood connecting with a human skull echoed in the room.

"Ooooow! Ma, what the heck! That really hurts!" John whined.

John and Jack saw the anger on Jena's face. She raised a giant wooden spoon and shook it at him. "You nearly made all of the food he just ate come back up with that stupid joke of yours." *Whack!*

"Ma, that really does hurt!" John cried out and rubbed his head.

"Good, now go and leave us be and take that mutt of yours out of here, too." Jena growled.

However, John stood defiant. "Nope, I'm staying right here."

"What?" Jena screeched. John ducked away from the third swipe of that wooden spoon and shot out the door.

"Jack, I'm right outside the door if you need me," John shouted.

Jack looked in the direction of his voice.

"Eat now, little one. He won't go far," Jena said with a soft, cooing voice.

Jack ate some more under the watchful eye of Jena Little Flower. Then she stepped out into another room, so he stopped to think about this whole situation. "Eat!" she scolded from the other room.

John slipped back in suddenly and sat beside him. "Little

Spirit, you've got to eat, or I'll bring your mother here so fast that . . ." Jack started to shovel in the food. John suddenly scrambled back out the door with Jena right behind him. She swung that giant spoon at him all the way out the door.

"I'm afraid I won't be able to keep him out for long. Blasted bullheaded man, he's just like his father." Jena sounded serious.

Jack took another bite of food in fear of that wooden spoon.

"He sure seems to like you a lot."

Jack spewed his food everywhere, choking.

John tumbled back into the room and accused his mother. "Ma, what did you do? Are you trying to make him choke?"

She laughed as she scurried into the other room.

Jack glanced up, transfixed on John.

John looked at him, and it took Jack's breath away for a second.

Jack gathered himself back to the real world. "There's a whole lot of things you don't know about and things we need to learn about each other if we're going to work together."

John smiled, and he covered Jack's hand with his. "I agree."

Whack! John went flying out the door again.

"You'll let that boy eat in peace!" she shouted at John. Then she then turned to Jack. "I told you he's interested in you," she said smugly and wagged that weapon of a spoon at him.

John came back to the table as Jack finished eating. He looked at John and said, "I'm finished eating, and I'm just exhausted." John again picked him up—Jack didn't protest as much this time. "I can walk, you know?" Again, Jack's heart melted at the smile appearing on John's face. He shuddered and nuzzled into John's chest.

John put him back in bed and pulled the covers up. Jack rolled away from him. "Where will you be sleeping, if I'm taking up your bed?" Jack asked.

Jena interceded. "He'll be on the couch, and I'll be in the guestroom next door, just in case you need something. As for that mutt of his, who knows where she'll be sleeping. Probably somewhere between you and John, so she can keep an eye on you both." John's mother smirked and walked out of the room.

Jack slept like a dead man.

Jack finally woke up himself somewhere around six the next morning. John's wolf sat in the room and glaring at him. She should have left Jack alone first thing in the morning. He yelled at her, "Get the hell out of here!"

"She yipped and flew out the door.

Jack mumbled, "What a sissy wolf."

John shot through the door. "What did you do to Bambi? Are you okay? Are you ready for breakfast? Do you need anything?" John bothered him before he could get himself fully awake.

That made Jack even grumpier. "I took myself off her menu. Fine. No. No, and get out! That's the answers to all your questions." Jack lay back down. Then he momentarily sat back up. "Sorry, I'm not a morning person."

Jack always woke up extremely grumpy, and it took a couple of cups of coffee and a while of no talking, no breathing out loud, and no touching, before he turned back into his sweet, adorable self again.

John left and within minutes, came back with coffee. Jack smelled the rich aroma and sat up in bed. "Ahhhh, nectar of the gods," Jack said. They sat in silence for fifteen minutes as Jack sipped his coffee.

The three medical ladies appeared with breakfast. "You'll eat this, and then we'll decide about your day," Jena announced as she raised her spoon.

"Yes, ma'am," Jack said.

She and John immediately started to argue. "You'll not hit him, Ma, and I mean it!"

"Now, did I hit him?" she asked and shook her spoon at him.

"No, but you threatened, and you can't do that either, not ever!" John stood there with his arms folded, ready for a fight.

"Okay, then, when I need to whack him a good one, I'll do you instead." She huffed at him.

Jack laughed at John and Jena. It was like watching a cartoon.

Jack decided to try his breakfast and ate what he could, which was way more than he normally ate in the morning. Jack figured that would have to suffice. He quickly learned differently when Jena returned.

"You'll not leave that chair until you've eaten a proper breakfast. Eat!" Jena planned to have her way.

"I really ate a lot. I'm full. Besides, I never eat breakfast." Jack told both Jena and John.

John stood between his mother and Jack. John's eyebrows started to knit into a stern expression on his face, as a warning to his mother.

"Ma, no hitting."

Jack ate some more in total silence. Jena smirked and left. John sat down beside him. Jack leaned into John and sniffed, and John's smell was almost intoxicating.

"Bambi's pissed," John said to Jack.

Jack responded, "I bet, and if she ever shows her one thousand sharp white teeth at me again, she may join the members of the dead endangered species list. She'd make a great throw rug."

"She's just possessive of me," John laughingly said.

"Guess that'd run most dates off then, huh?" Jack snidely remarked.

John laughed out loud.

"I'd never date anyone that has a wolf for a mate," Jack took another bite of his breakfast.

"She's a friend and companion, and she comes and goes at will. Sometimes, I don't see her for months."

Jack quipped, "So how did this on-again-off-again relationship start?"

"There's no relationship! I raised her from a cub. She thinks I'm pack."

Jack looked at John. "I'll have to keep an eyeball peeled. Hell hath no fury, as they say," Jack teasingly said. John frowned. Jack smirked at him even more. "You're just so easy."

Chapter Three

Finally, overly protective Jena let Jack off bed confinement because he'd eaten all of his breakfast. But in actuality, John helped him some by eating anything Jack left on the plate.

Jack asked John to leave the room so he could dress in his clothes that someone had laid out for him. John very coyly said, "I thought I'd stay and help you dress, you being in a weakened condition and all."

Jack just rolled his eyes. "Not a chance, big boy. Out!"

John returned twenty minutes later. Jack had cleaned up, dressed, and was ready to go.

He explained to Jack about the plans for the day. "We, well, at least I need to go to the school to see what's happening, and you should probably come, too."

"Duh, like I'd let you go there without me. I'm the school administrator, after all." Jack smiled at John.

"We'll come back for lunch and then plan the rest of the day, if that's okay?"

"Do I have a choice?" Jack asked.

"No," Jena said ever so flatly. She glared first at John, then softened a little as she turned to Jack. Jena made things abundantly clear. "Little Spirit's due back for lunch." Jena gave John a look that would almost certainly frighten even the strongest of men. "Do you understand this, son, or do I need to get the wooden spoon?"

They both nodded they understood.

"I got it, Ma, nothing too strenuous, I promise. You know,

Ma, you gotta stop hitting people with that spoon. I've two major knots on my head. You could've given me a concussion or even brain damage."

"I'll show you brain damage!" Jena scurried off to seek out her weapon of choice.

John grabbed Jack's hand. "Let's get out of here before she kills me." Off they fled with Jack laughing at the ridiculousness of the situation. They heard Jena chuckling in the background.

Once they escaped, they slowed their pace and walked toward the school. It was just a few blocks away. When they neared the school, they witnessed a flurry of activity. Trucks drove in quickly and unloaded. Then men and women hauled large and small boxes into the building.

Jack turned to John. "Maybe they're unloading the missing computers, toilets, urinals, and other essential supplies."

John nodded in agreement. "I'll bet you're right!"

Jack noticed Hank all hot and sweaty, and he looked a little harried. There was a small woman giving out directions to the people working with them. She seemed to keep things moving in an orderly fashion.

"Who's that?" Jack nodded toward the women.

"She's my sister, Clair Spotted Fawn, and Hank's wife. She's got everyone working, that's for sure. She's bossy, just like Ma."

"She has some of the same beautiful features that you and your mother have."

John broke into a smile.

At that very moment, Big Chief Ass for a Face noticed them and approached. "I know you think I'm a piece of shit, and I deserve that, but I couldn't find one person that knows how to connect this computer stuff. John usually does that for everyone. Can you please help me, John? Little Spirit? Please?"

John whispered in Jack's ear, "You know that you don't

have to if you don't want to, right?"

"Yes, I do. I want my school ready," Jack said as he stepped away from John and headed into the building. He walked through crowds of people as they painted, scrubbed, and hauled boxes.

Jack stopped and looked at the painted section of wall. His face went from a giant smile to a very unhappy frown. Clearing his throat, he flatly stated, "That's the ugliest baby shit green paint I've ever seen, and it's a big no!" About ten painters stopped their work and applauded. He turned to John, who'd caught up with him. "John, who in the hell picked out that paint?"

The people in the room all said at the same time, "Hank Flying Crow because it's cheap."

Administrator Jack came to life. "We'll have shades of blue, and it must be certified child safe. I'm glad you haven't done much." He spotted Donna and waved her over to him. "Donna, will you take care of this paint issue for me, please? And we need the paint like yesterday."

She smiled and winked at him, then trundled off.

They'd unpacked and set most computers up on the computer tables. All Jack had to do was connect them, set up the server, and get them all online. Then he'd need to download the new educational programs on all ninety of them, and in only two and a half days. "It'll be challenging, but doable," he proclaimed as he stepped into the lab and got to work.

John left Jack and started with the server. He'd informed Jack he knew exactly what to do.

Jack connected the computers in the labs one at a time. Donna set up the computers in the office and staff room. A man who introduced himself as Daniel Falling Star volunteered to work on the computers in the library.

Hank and his crew finished hauling in all the computers and quickly moved to the other things that needed to be brought in and connected.

Jack worked tirelessly. He connected the computers, and time just slipped away.

There was a very loud commotion out in the hall, and everyone stepped out to see what caused the commotion. Jack looked at his watch. The morning really had flown by, and it was after one already.

Ma Jena, with her heavy spoon in hand, pointed at John. "Where's Little Spirit? He needs to eat."

Donna came from behind the office desk and stepped up to her mother. "Ma! That's enough of your bullying ways. Put that spoon down. We've been working our fingers raw here. Why didn't you just bring lunch here to all these starving people?" She stood defiantly and glared at her mother. They looked almost like twins as they squinted, trying to stare each other down.

"Silly girl," Jena said and pointed, as twenty or so women carried in what looked to be enough food for the entire state of North Dakota. "Everyone stops and eats now!" Jena stated, as she banged that huge spoon on the front office desk. Donna hugged her mother, and they joined in and helped set up the food in the cafeteria.

Everyone filled their plates, sat, and ate. Talk and laughter filled the room. People chattered away, told stories, and shared news of what went on around the reservation. Jack heard someone say to Jena, "Didn't Doc tell that frail little thing not to have babies?"

John told Jack stories about the history of the Lakota Nation and their people. Jack listened intently to what John was saying, until he inadvertently noticed Hank sitting alone at a distant table. Jack politely held up his index finger and requested John pause for one second.

Jack got up and walked over to Hank. The room went silent. "Hank, come and join us. We need to discuss some school matters with you." Hank sat stunned, then looked around, stood up, and followed Jack over to his table. The laughter and chatter started up just where it'd left off.

John leaned toward Hank. "You know Hank, Little Spirit helped you save face just now?"

Hank nodded and looked at Jack. "Thanks, Little Spirit."

Jack smiled. "Apology accepted. Let's move on. Hank, the playground equipment here's very old and run down and looks to be dangerous. Can you and your crew rebuild it before school opens?"

Hank huffed back at Jack. "It's just fine. That shit's been here for years and was perfectly good for us, and it's perfectly good for our kids."

"Have you totally lost your mind? That stuff out there's really dangerous and won't pass inspection."

Hank stood. "It's just fine."

Jack stood up, too, and he looked like he was ready to spring at Hank, but John quickly got between them.

Feeling overly confident with John between them, Hank said rudely to Jack, "You're full of it."

Whack! Ma Jena to the rescue. Hank yelped like a stepped-on puppy, sat down, and rubbed his aching head.

"Replace the equipment, understood? Child safety always comes first."

"Got it," he responded, and she turned and started to walk away, until Hank mumbled, *"Ye' káŋ kȟaŋǧí."*

Jena froze in mid-step and did a pivot turn. Fire lit in her eyes. She'd heard his remark, and she twirled and charged the table. Hank got up and took off with Jena in hot pursuit.

John sat back and shook his head, looking as though he was trying to squelch his laughter. Jack looked to him for translation. "He called her an old crow. Big mistake. Some things won't ever change. So you know the reality of the situation, Hank will always argue about any change, or how to spend money, and Ma will always carry that spoon." The entire table laughed out loud.

Jack smiled and said to himself, "I think maybe I'm finding a home here." He caught John's gaze at that exact moment, and John's face lit up, his eyes sparkled, and he smiled warmly and tenderly at Jack.

The people at the table looked at Jack, then John, and they all smiled a knowing smile at each other.

Everyone went back to work. Donna found Jack and told him that the paint had arrived, and the painters applied a small sample of it on the wall for his approval. The shades of complementary blue proved to be just beautiful. The flowing pattern that looked like rolling waves looked perfect for the school. Jack just stared in silence. Everyone waited for his reaction.

Finally, John had to ask, "Well, Little Spirit, don't you like it?"

"It's magnificent!" he told them all. John pulled him in for a hug.

A happy "Yes!" sounded from the painters.

Everyone worked day and night for the next day and a half. They painted, installed, took down, and replaced. The building looked like a brand new place for learning, and more importantly, because everyone got involved, it came together quickly.

This school was just about ready for the big inspection.

Only one incident arose during the entire renovation. Jack thought the bison heads should be taken down. Hank went apeshit crazy, and several other tribe members protested, too.

John rounded the corner and asked, "What's all this commotion about?" They all spoke at once and told him about the bison. John frowned, and his attention turned to Jack. "There isn't much I'll deny you, Little Spirit, but the *ptéȟčaka*, the bison stay. They're symbols of our culture and way of life. Each is here hanging for a reason, which I'll explain at another time. So hear me. They stay." John spoke gently but assertively.

Jack paused for a moment, then nodded without protest, but added, "Don't you think they all should be at least vacuumed?" The others stood there and just gaped at Jack. "What? They've got to be very dusty from hanging there for these years."

After a pregnant pause, one of the men said, "Get me a damn vacuum cleaner. He's right about them being huge dust collectors."

With the incident over, everyone returned to their duties and worked steadily to complete the school. All the while, Jena and her sisters watched over, fed, and took care of Jack. John was never far away and always spoke sweetly to him.

At the end of the day, Jack felt exhausted. He sure dreaded another night on the couch.

John escorted him home and urged Jack to go look in his bedroom. He opened the door wide, and much to his surprise, he found his new bed all set up and made.

"What a wonderful surprise," Jack said as he turned to John. "When on earth did you have time to do this?" Jack asked.

John just smiled and shrugged his shoulders.

Jack immediately stepped up and hugged him. "Thank you so much."

Although school hadn't started, Jack still needed to go to work every day. There was much that still needed to be done, and Jack had to prepare the necessary paperwork for the inspection.

John appeared at Jack's door early every morning. He knocked and waited for Jack to open it. Jack would snarl at him. John always had a huge mug of strong black coffee and something for Jack to eat. Grumpy Jack disappeared by the time they started to leave for school. John walked him to the school daily, and Jack chattered away, like a happy little ground squirrel, about all the completed tasks and the few things yet to be done. Jack had always detested mornings, but they seemed to be easier to cope with John around.

Jack's brother Jason laughed loud and long when Jack said, "I'm not a morning person . . . but having John close by makes it somewhat nicer and easier to take."

Jason joked, "I'm surprised poor John's still alive."

The state inspection went off without a hitch. The committee gave Jack and the council a very positive verbal report. They told Jack and the chiefs that they would make a decision and let them know the results as soon as possible. The committee said their goodbyes and left.

Later that night, Jack was busily unpacking the things that the movers had delivered a couple of days prior, but he hadn't found the time to unpack much of anything. So he started the monumental task. Boxes were opened, and packing paper filled the rooms.

In the middle of this mess, someone knocked at his door, "Just a minute," Jack hollered, but whoever knocked now knocked louder and more rapidly, making it impossible for Jack to be heard. Jack flung open the door. "What the hell's the emergency?" Jack barked. There stood John with his face laced with major concern and worry.

"When you didn't answer the door, I nearly broke it down," John said.

Jack looked at the massive, solid wood door and chuckled, and looked back at John. "Yeah, right. Anyway, I was busy and had my hands full. Do you need something?" Jack sounded slightly annoyed.

"I came to help you. You know something, if you lose that nasty attitude and clean up that filthy mouth, you'd be even cuter," John said with a smile, which made Jack flush.

"Really?" Jack asked sarcastically.

John nodded without expression.

Jack realized he'd come across rather abruptly. "Okay, I'm sorry. Do you really want to help?"

John nodded.

"Then could you please unpack the kitchen stuff? I can put all the stuff away after you unpack it. I know just where I want to put everything. Doing that would really help me out."

"Aww, dang, I was hoping to be able to go through your personal things," John said, and he waggled his eyebrows.

Jack laughed. "Not a chance!" Jack twirled him around and sent him in the direction of the kitchen. Jack went back and worked in bedrooms and baths while John worked in the kitchen.

About an hour later, John strolled into Jack's bedroom and asked what else he needed him to do. Jack froze and just blankly stared at John. Annoyed, he said to John, "If you're not going to help me, then please go home." Jack marched to the kitchen. "You could've at least —" Jack froze in his tracks. All the drawers and cupboards lay open. Not only had John unpacked everything, but he'd also put it all away precisely the way Jack had planned for it to be. Plus, John had cleaned up all the unpacking mess. Jack barked in surprise, "Holy shit!" Then he stood moving his mouth but with nothing coming out.

"Little Spirit, you got this fish mouth thing going on. It's kind of freaking me out," John said as his index finger twirled in a small circle in front of Jack's face.

"How in the heck did you do all of this in an hour?" Jack

asked him.

John said with the utmost sincerity, "I'm a trained Lakota warrior. I know how to focus and not be distracted. You're like a little mouse running from place to place to place."

"Are you sure you didn't sneak in help?" Jack asked warily. "You had to have help, and how could've you had even the slightest idea of how I wanted this place set up?" Jack waited to get John's response.

"Oh, that part was easy. I just read your thoughts." John smiled that wonderful smile, and it distracted Jack for a moment. He stood there looking at John with both amazement and adoration.

"I think I ought to marry you right here and now." Jack smiled, and both stepped closer.

The moment was halted because Jack's phone started ringing. They both heard it. The two of them looked startled. Then Jack started a panicked search for his phone.

John stood and watched him until, finally, Jack asked, "Are you kidding me? Are you going to help me or what? This could be the inspection results."

"Sure, it's over there under the papers on the coffee table." John pointed across the room. Jack doubted it, but when he lifted the papers, there sat his phone. Jack gave him the *how-in-the-hell* look.

"Answer the dang phone!" John said, bringing Jack back into focus.

"Hello, Dr. Jackson McIntire speaking."

"Hello Dr. McIntire, it's Dr. Sammuelson."

"Hello, Dr. Sammuelson."

"I wanted to call you myself with the inspection results. Is now a good time?".

"Yes, sir."

"You must be so proud of your new school."

"Yes, sir."

"I'm so excited to report that your school passed the inspection with flying colors in all areas. You excelled, congratulations!"

"Thank you."

"Your school is now certified."

"Oh, that's so wonderful."

"Congratulations. I hope you have a wonderful year. Take care."

"Yes, sir, and the same to you. Thank you so much. Good-bye, Dr. Sammuelson."

"Good-bye."

Jack stood there and stared at his phone. The pause lasted too long.

"Well?" John finally asked.

It hit Jack like a bullet between the eyes. "Oh my God! We passed!" He screamed at the top of his lungs just like a little kid, then danced around in circles. "We surpassed all expectations! John, we're a certified school!" They danced around like two crazy men, laughing and whooping it up.

John threw open the front door and shouted something in Lakota to the world outside. Suddenly, adults with their children started to appear from out of nowhere. The word spread like wildfire, and more and more people arrived. Everyone there congratulated Jack, John, and each other.

The entire group moved to the enormous Council Hall. Food and people came out of nowhere. Dozens and dozens of children raced and chased and scurried from one place to another. Babies, in seats, lined up in a huge semi-circle. Jack stopped and talked to and cooed to each one.

Standing around and chatting with Jena, Jack suddenly noticed that John and Hank were arguing off to the side of the room. They both looked way too angry. Some of the council members walked up to thank Jack for his excellent work. Jack nodded in the direction of Hank and John, then asked Jena,

"Can you please referee that out?"

Off she went to deal with that situation. She stepped between them, and the whole thing ended quickly.

A few seconds later, he felt an arm slip around his waist. It was John. "No fair dogging us out with Ma," he whispered as he kissed Jack's ear.

In that instance, Jack realized John had just outed them both to his entire tribe, and now everyone knew that a relationship between them could be budding. Jack scanned the room. Not everyone looked friendly. He saw some tense facial expressions, but John acted normally. Jack looked at him, and John smiled. Jack smiled back and leaned into John.

John proved right about Hank—he argued about every detail. He could get cheaper paint, but it might be harmful to the kids. He'd clean the school for less money than the janitorial staff could. However, his wife pointed out that he never knew to put his dirty underwear in the laundry basket. Hank demonstrated over and over what a cheap-ass bastard acted like, but he did know money and how to pinch a *nickel until the buffalo shit*. Something Thomas had said several times. Plus, some of the deals he found were more than spectacular, for example he got one hundred new school desks for less than half of the listed price.

Right before school started, the school board planned a meeting. Jack gathered a list of unfinished things he thought would be nice for the school, most of them for safety reasons, but some for aesthetic purposes. Hank tried to shoot down every point as unnecessary or too expensive. Hank mostly lost but won on the planting of trees, shrubs, and flowers around the school. Hank argued it would just give vermin a place to hide and that it took away the look of their prairie school—the board agreed with him. Jack settled back in his chair and said to John, "Just can't win them all."

CHAPTER FOUR

The first day teachers returned to start their new school year, John, Donna, and Jack walked around the school to introduce Jack to the staff. Until then, Jack had been so busy that there wasn't time to be formally introduced. The very first introduction turned out to be Helen Gordon. A beautiful woman, tall, statuesque, and full-figured, she had thick blonde hair and light gray eyes. However, she wasn't very friendly toward Jack. She had a hateful glare she laid on him, which made him uncomfortable. She only answered questions Jack asked her directly with no further details or comments.

As they got out of Helen's earshot, Jack turned to Donna Yellow Bird and asked, "What's with her?"

"Her mother's a member of the tribe, but not her father, and he died in the Gulf War. And just so you know, Helen had her sights set on John. It'd become obvious to everyone that John was like stupidly interested in you. However, it wasn't until she saw you two together that it became a reality."

John winced at what Donna said, and Jack noticed his reaction. When John stepped over to talk to one of the people cleaning, Jack whispered to Donna, "John seems like the kind of man that can't stand it when someone hurts because of him."

Donna nodded and added, "Big heart and gentle spirit."

Jack found the love interest thing funny and odd. Donna felt the same, and the two of them laughed like a pair of monkeys about the whole situation, but never when John was around.

Jack's curiosity spiked. "Donna, didn't Helen know John's gay?"

Donna sort of chuckled and told him, "Sure. But she planned on converting him, I think." Both Jack and Donna froze for a second, and Jack just shook his head.

"Sad." They both said.

Donna told Jack that Helen was an excellent 5th-grade teacher nevertheless.

Jack smiled and told Donna, "I hope she proves to be just that, so I can find a good reason to like her, despite her un-friendliness."

They wandered around and visited with each of the teachers in his or her room. Donna quietly filled him in on the staff, with John's help, of course. Robert Red Fox, the kindergarten teacher, looked a lot like Ichabod Crane, the one from the cartoon, but he presented himself just so sweetly. He and his wife were expecting their fourth son in a couple of weeks.

Donna said, "He loves the kids, and they love him, and he handles twenty-two kindergarteners with ease."

Jack, John, and Donna continued, and as they rounded the corner, they ran into two teachers who were in the midst of a very private conversation and were holding hands. They immediately stopped when they saw the trio headed in their direction.

Donna introduced them. It was an awkward introduction as they stumbled over their words and worked far too hard trying not to look at each other. Jack noticed it immediately. Mike Turtle and Mina White Clover were obviously very much in love.

The two of them were reasonably good-looking and tried very hard to be friendly. Both were full-blooded Lakota and openly expressed their pride in that fact. Their classrooms were located next door to each other, which seemed weird to Jack. Mike taught the eighth-grade classes, and Mina, first-grade.

With introductions over, the three of them moved on. Donna then filled Jack in on the pair as they moved on to meet the next teacher. "Every chance they could, they'd sneak off and spend time together. They've been pretending not to be involved for a couple of years now. Why I don't know, they make a cute couple."

Jack said to both John and Donna, "I've noted to move the classrooms so they're clustered together, like K, one, two and three, four, five, and so on." He handed it to Donna.

She glanced at the memo and smiled her approval.

John pointed out Jesse Swift Comet, who taught the seventh graders. Jack saw he was talking to another man. Donna informed him that it was his partner, Jorge Peraz, who taught the second grade. They'd lived together for fifteen years. The two of them had earned the respect and love of the tribe.

Donna continued, "It wasn't always the case, and the pair endured some very abusive treatment at times when they first started to live together here on the reservation. But time and their dedication to our children turned that around."

They met and shook hands and chatted for a few minutes.

Jack commented as they walked down the hallway, "They're so friendly and personable. I'm going to bet they're really wonderful teachers."

The three of them moved on to the next classroom, where a pretty young woman was busy working.

"Six years ago, Sally Anne Houston came to do her student teaching at the school and just never left," John whispered to Jack. "She's hopelessly in love with Donna. Sally Anne teaches the sixth grade."

The way Donna stood and gazed at her, Jack realized that Donna probably felt the same about Sally Anne, even if they presented as opposite ends of the spectrum, Donna round and dark, and Sally Anne lean and fair. As they left the room, Jack said to John, "They make a nice couple, don't they?"

John smiled and nodded.

The fourth-grade teacher named Ida Wild Rose looked to be about a hundred years old, but she still moved spryly around the room. She smiled easily and laughed loudly.

Donna told Jack that she'd just turned seventy years old and absolutely refused to retire. Her own kids begged her to quit so she could spend more time with her grandkids, but she wanted none of that. *"I'm going to die in my teacher's chair in my classroom,"* Donna quoted Ida Wild Rose.

"That scares me a little," Jack whispered to John and Donna, who both agreed.

Then a tiny woman with maroon hair and green eyes stepped out of the next classroom and introduced herself. "Hi, I'm Tina Marie O'Ryan Wolf, third-grade teacher and married to Paul Wolf. You've met him. He's a member of the Tribal Council. You look a little frazzled. You need a hug." Hug him, she did.

Jack smiled and said, "I'm so pleased to meet you, too." They chatted a moment and moved on.

Donna described her, "She's a tiny spitfire, that one. She keeps that husband and her three kids in tow. She's also a big hugger, as you may have noticed."

Once the elementary school introductions were completed, it was time for the high school.

Donna had been so helpful with information about each person. Jack told her how much he appreciated it, which, of course, ended with a big hug.

Not to be left out, John asked, "How about me?"

Jack got more than just a friendly hug from John.

Donna put a stop to that right away. "Hey! Stop that! We're

in a public place." Both men separated and looked a bit sheepish. "Go home if you need some alone time," Donna laughingly said to the two of them.

On their way to the high school section of the school, they passed by the office, and the phones were ringing off the hook. Several people stood in the office, plus the answering machine was flashing. Donna told them to go ahead without her, as she really needed to be in the office for a while to take care of some school business.

The men started to leave when Jack stopped and popped his head back into the front office. "Donna, announce to the teachers not to decorate their rooms just yet. Tell them there'll be some classroom shifting."

Donna smiled and did a thumbs-up.

"John, our school is in the shape of the capital letter *I* and ends sort forming a giant *T*. The central hallway divides the end wings. The office is in the middle, with the cafeteria close to the elementary part and the gym close to the high school. I'm going to move preschool through fourth grade to the left side of the *T*, and at the right side will be the upper elementary. That way, the upper grades can interchange subjects if needed. It would be more like a middle school. Because of the labs, the high school has to stay the way it is. What'd you think about that idea?"

John thought for a second. "Little Spirit, I like the way you're always planning to make the most of this school for our children. I think that's a great idea."

John stepped up to do the introductions. He walked Jack over to the high school section. The high school had only eight teachers. Only a couple of them were working diligently in their classrooms—the others were playing touch football outside.

"There's time for games?" He gave John a questioning look that turned to a look of disgust.

John clearly got the message that Jack found this unacceptable. Thank goodness Donna rejoined them. John excused himself, and she took Jack to meet the teachers who were in their rooms working.

Priscilla Grafton taught all the sciences—physical science, biology, chemistry, and physics. She was articulate and presented herself as brilliant and charming. She and her husband, Del, had moved there twenty years ago on a federal grant and decided to stay. He taught French and all the English courses. They both charmed Jack with their candor and wonderful humor. They invited Jack to come to dinner in the near future. Jack, of course, said he'd love that.

Jasper Spotted Horse taught the history and government classes. Even though quite good-looking, he came across as timid and shy. He smiled all the time and nervously bit his nails.

Jack said "With the school opening in just a few days, I'm a bit surprised you and the others decided to play ball instead of working."

"I promise I'll be ready, Dr. McIntire," Jasper said and immediately got to work on his room.

As they moved on to the next room, Donna scolded Jack, "You nearly made that man poop his pants. You saw that he's very shy. Shame on you."

Jack replied, "True, but I'll bet his classroom and lesson plans will be ready in no time."

John rejoined them.

Next, Jack met Jean-Paul DuBois, the physical education teacher and sports coach. He was married to one of John's sisters, Kitten Blue Bird. Kitten ran the cafeteria, and she'd earned a degree in nutrition. She also taught home economics classes. Jack had met her earlier at Jena's home. Jean-Paul strutted over to the trio.

Jack didn't show any annoyance, he simply asked Jean-

Paul, "So you're ready to show me your lesson plans for the first day of school?"

"Lesson plans? Are you kidding? I don't do lesson plans. I coach, man. Didn't they tell you that? Who's this guy?"

Jack bristled just a little. "I'm Dr. Jackson McIntire, the new school administrator. I was hired to have this school in compliance with state standards so it can become a fully accredited school. It doesn't matter what a person teaches or how important anyone *thinks* they are ... every person on this teaching staff will do lesson plans, meet with me weekly, and comply with the teaching standards of the state and this school. If anyone doesn't like that or isn't able to meet these requirements, resignations will be accepted all day. Any questions ... coach?" Jack spoke curtly but still acted totally professional.

Jean-Paul paled a bit, then nodded that he got the message.

Jack moved on to the next classroom.

John moved up into his face. "Jean-Paul, I hope you realized that was Little Spirit, Dr. Jackson McIntire, our school administrator?"

"Shit, I do now," Jean-Paul grumbled. "Kitten's going to kill me."

John scoffed. "Kitten's the least of your worries, Ma's become Little Spirit's self-appointed protector, and she's—" Before he could finish, Jena appeared like a ghost out of nowhere. She pounced on Jean-Paul like a cougar. He scrambled off with Ma Jena hot on his heels.

In the next room, behaving as though nothing had transpired just minutes before, Jack was being a professional all the way. John stood there ogling Jack. The passionate gaze gave him away.

Donna noticed and elbowed him, then said in her quiet, soft-spoken voice, "John, put your drooling tongue away. Everyone's already aware that you're falling in love. You require a private room anytime you're around Dr. McIntire. Use some decorum around him, okay? After all, he's the new school administrator, and we want to keep him." John shot her a guilty look. Donna pointed and laughed at him the way only a sister could.

The whole situation helped Jack feel more comfortable in the new school.

The next day, very early in the morning, John knocked on Little Spirit's door. "Come on, Jack. I need to show you around your new home."

Jack opened his door, he had an *I-am–going-to-kill-you* look on his face, and his hair was in total disarray. John, with his best heart-melting smile, handed him a super-sized cup of piping hot coffee.

Jack growled at John and said, "Don't speak, don't breathe, don't even move a muscle until I've had this cup, or I might bite your head off. I stayed up very late last night working on school stuff."

John silently sat down and waited for grumpy, mean, and bitey Jack to disappear and for sweet Jack to come forth. John got restless and went ahead and started a fresh pot of coffee as a backup.

Finally, Jack looked at him. "What on earth are you doing here at the ass crack of dawn? The children start school on Monday, and seeing this is Saturday, I'd planned to sleep in a little and then go to the school and work." Jack was still slightly grumpy, but not so grumpy that he'd chew off John's arm.

As he poured Jack more coffee, John said, "First of all, that grouchy mouth, stop already! Little Spirit, I thought it'd be important for you to learn about the different things that go on here and about the places that the children will talk about when school starts."

John grabbed Jack's attention. "Such as?"

"The bison herd, the ancient sacred grounds, and I'd like you to see how and where we live. With everything that needed to be done to start up the school, you haven't had a chance to see any of these things."

Jack smiled and said, "All I can say is you're right. That'd be such a wonderful experience."

Jack got up and moved toward his bedroom. John stood and started to follow him.

"You stay here and mind the fort while I get dressed."

John felt sheepishly disappointed, but he sat back down on the sofa.

Jack talked loud enough for John to hear him as he dressed in his bedroom. He asked questions about the things they'd see. When they left his house and John helped him into his jeep, Jack said, "I'm disappointed that we won't be riding around on a pair of painted mustang horses."

John found this very humorous and laughed as he told Jack, "Little Spirit, there are hundreds of thousands of acres on the reservation. You wouldn't be able to walk for a week if we rode all day on horseback." John laughed even more at the thought of riding horseback. However, one look at Jack, and the urge to laugh disappeared. John thought it best not to poke a waking bear.

By the time they reached the bison herd, Jack had started acting almost like a little kid — he bounced around in his seat with excitement. He seemed awe-struck looking around. Suddenly, without warning, the bison appeared in front of them.

John stopped the jeep. Jack immediately darted out of the vehicle and set up his camera. Unfortunately, he moved around too quickly in the direction of the herd. Several of the bull bison took that to be a challenge and charged. John watched as Jack saw what was happening through his camera lens, but instead of hightailing it back to the jeep, he just froze. The fact that six one-ton bovines charged at him obviously made his brain and body unable to function. John swooped in, pulling him into the jeep before the big guys got to him.

Jack looked at John. "How'd you do that, coming out of nowhere and then rescuing me?"

John just smiled. "I'm a trained Lakota warrior."

Jack mumbled a thank you, but John wanted to hear him say it louder. "I'm sorry, Little Spirit, did you say something?"

Jack caved and responded, "Thank you for saving my life, but for God's sake, never tell my mother."

John raised his right hand. "Warrior's honor."

They moved to the part of the reservation where the tribe made most of the products they used on the reservation and the other things they sold. A working tannery sat on the edge of the compound. It smelled like rotting flesh and chemicals. Jack wrinkled his nose and said, "Phew! No wonder it's at the edge of this enormous compound." John and Jack wandered through one of the buildings where people were working. They made leather clothes—both ceremonial for the people here and other things they sold to the public. He chatted with the workers and praised them for their beautiful work.

John enjoyed watching Jack, who stood in awe as people in the next building sewed the very intricate beadwork right onto the leather clothing and onto the other magnificent things they made—toys, headdresses, and belts, plus much more.

The tour continued. Everywhere they went, the workers stopped work and spoke with the man they called Little Spirit.

Jack's charm and genuine interest in what was happening made the people comfortable with him.

Screaming Eagle noticed them and walked over and stood

next to John and said, "His loving nature and gentleness with the children is making everyone like him so much."

John's radiant smile showed how much his heart soared. "I figured that would happen."

Moving on to the next area of the reservation, they rode past places that looked like smaller villages. The adults worked, and children played outside. Every time they came upon these housing developments, the children waved as the jeep passed by.

John observed that Jack still lacked an understanding of the significance of his name, Little Spirit. Nothing in his demeanor showed anything but how much he loved children and enjoyed meeting everyone. One day, he'd understand the importance of being Little Spirit.

When they passed through a herd of horses, Jack became completely awestruck. "How many of them are there?" he asked.

"Around a hundred and fifty. They belong to the entire tribe," John answered him.

Jack took dozens of pictures. As they swung back toward home, they once again met the herd of bison. Jack asked about the makeup of the herd and how John's people kept predation down.

"Little Spirit, the herd belongs to the Great Father. He gave us this land and the herd of bison. He expects us to share and yet still protect our gifts from him. So if we lose a few sickly or stupid animals, then it just makes the herd stronger and healthier."

Jack pointed toward the herd. "John, look at what's happening!" Excitement sounded in Jack's voice. John looked out and saw a relatively large pack of wolves as they barreled down the hill directly toward the herd.

John knew they needed to get out of the herd's way. "Hold on tight!" John shouted and took off like a bat out of hell, just ahead of the herd. Little Spirit turned around with his knees in the seat and watched the commotion. John pulled behind a rocky outcrop, and they got out and watched from on top of the rocks as the herd separated and moved around them.

"John, this is so incredibly amazing!" Jack shouted.

John watched Little Spirit's expression to see how he would react when the wolves took down a young, limping bison. It surprised him a bit when Jack cheered for the wolves. With the hunt over, Jack turned to John. "That was the most incredible thing I've ever seen in my life. Shit, I mean, shoot, I forgot to turn on my camera!" John threw his head back and laughed out loud. Even Jack eventually found the humor in it.

"That mouth of yours, work on it, please," John told him, and Jack blushed red. Jack raised his hand and vowed, "I promise it won't happen again."

John struggled to contain his laughter.

"You can stop that internal laughter. Okay, I promise to try very hard not to let it happen anymore. How's that?"

John reached for Jack and pulled him close. "You're something very special, Jackson McIntire."

Jack and John explored the entire reservation many times over the next few weeks and met so many people. Jack told Donna how much he looked forward to every excursion with John.

Donna's gaze sparkled with delight. "Is it because you like to see all the things on the reservation or because you're with John?"

Jack blushed. "Both!"

Donna hugged him tightly.

Chapter Five

Days after the children arrived, Jack summoned the faculty for a meeting after school. He planned to discuss how things have been going so far with the faculty and staff. But when he entered the gym to start his meeting, he stopped and looked shocked. There sat the entire council, as well as dozens the parents and grandparents. The small faculty meeting that he'd planned turned into a huge surprise meeting. He shot John a look. John shrugged, then looked a little sheepish.

None of that mattered. Jack needed to discuss the curriculum and go over the schedules and all the new rules and regulations once again. So he just continued with what was on his agenda. He first presented the expectations to the staff that the state boards of education had given them. Teachers and some parents huffed about it, but when Jack explained that it kept them accredited and thus open, they seemed to back down and got quiet.

Jack then laid out all his expectations and his procedures. Again, he heard grumbling, mostly from the faculty. That, of course, did nothing to change what Jack had planned. Finally, he started his prepared speech. He had told John that he dreaded this most. His goal was to fire up his staff and get them excited about making the school successful.

"Okay, ladies and gentlemen, I want you to know how proud I am to be here at this school. We've high expectations to be met, but from what I've been told and observed, you're the best faculty, the most diligent of teachers, and the most caring of people. Our children will grow, learn, and excel because of your fine abilities. I promise you this, here and now. Nothing will be added to your workload that isn't essential to keeping this school up and running and accredited. I'm asking you to help me guide the children of the Native American Independent Nation of the Black Mountain Lakota Reservation to be the best they can be and even go beyond what we believe they can accomplish."

For just a second, it remained silent. Then the applause thundered all around him. Even though it startled him a little, he looked at John, and John just smiled broadly.

Suddenly, the entire staff surrounded Jack. They sang and danced. Jack felt John's arm as it encircled his waist. John stood dewy-eyed as he smiled at Little Spirit. Jack stepped in closer, and the dancing crowd grew and grew.

John shouted in his ear, "They're celebrating the coming of the new school year, but mostly they're welcoming you to our nation. Be proud, my Little Spirit. Because of your determination to better the education of the children and because you've made such an effort to get to know everyone, they're falling in love with you, too."

"*Too*?" Jack mouthed. He looked right into John's eyes and saw love there.

The dancing abruptly stopped, and the crowd separated. Chief Thomas Three Elks appeared in front of Jack, and alongside him, his wife, Jena Little Flower, followed by the rest of the chief's council. The powerful chief raised his hand, and the room became instantly still and silent. Jena raised the small spear she held in her hand and spoke in Lakota. It didn't take Jack long to realize she was praying, and so he began to bow his head. John nudged him and raised his head higher, indicating for him not to bow his head. Jack complied.

The ceremony came to completion when Jena handed the small spear-shaped object to Chief Thomas, who in turn then gave it to Jack, saying, "*Le' ktA ya okhophesniyan.*"

John whispered, "This will keep you safe."

He took the spear, and Chief Thomas gently wrapped his hand around Jack's to steady them. "Dr. Jackson Lee McIntire, you're Little Spirit, *Mithakos*."

Jack looked at John. "*Mithakos*?" He saw the shocked look on John's face and decided the meaning of that word could come later. The crowd once again broke into celebration. Everyone danced and sang. After an hour or so, the people began to disperse. They went back to their daily routines, and the staff went back to work in the classrooms.

Later that night, when John walked Jack home, he said what *mithakos* meant. "It means something like my child-in-law."

"John, why does your family act like we're married or something?" Jack casually asked him.

"My gosh, Little Spirit, it's because you've grabbed my heart and are now holding it hostage." He then kissed Jack, and Jack kissed him back.

Later that night, Jack called his brother Jason. "I've been here for just a few weeks, and I'm pretty sure I'm already falling in love. I hope this isn't a huge mistake."

Jason just warned, "Jack, this time, be careful with your heart, but don't be afraid to follow it. Only this time, also follow what your brain's telling you, not just your heart."

The new school year was off to a great start. Everything just fell into place. There were so many wonderful comments about the beautiful interior and the perfect placement of the classrooms. Parents filled the volunteers' lists, and students quickly moved into the routine of the school day.

Jack discovered in the days that followed that these people held close many secrets. Most of the time, he only discovered them by accident. He noted that sometimes when a child got very angry, his or her eye color changed. Their eyes, which were usually a dark brown, turned deep black, and their pupils disappeared. It sounded wildly crazy, but he saw it multiple times. Each time it happened, an adult appeared, and they took the child's hand and went for a walk. He didn't know what they said, but it worked, and the child came back happy, with his or her anger gone. He asked John and Donna about it, and they suggested that Jack got overly emotional and sappy about the children in his care. Jack told them both, "I feel like I'm not privy to some things. It isn't a bad feeling but one of mystery."

Something else that Jack noticed was the children called nearly all adults and elderly people Aunt or Uncle or Grandfather or Grandmother. The adults followed this pattern, too. Jack was somewhat perplexed by this, so he finally asked John about it. "Is everyone here on the reservation that closely related?"

A chuckle burst out of John, but when he caught the expression on Jack's face, he said, "Little Spirit, the entire Lakota Nation's a huge family. So everyone's an honorary aunt, uncle, or grandparent to everyone else, and the children are all each other's cousins. It not only shows respect but symbolizes the close bond we keep as a nation and that every adult's responsible in some way to help raise our children."

"Wow!" After a minute, Jack took John's hand. "You know, I get that, my parents have some very close friends, and my brothers and sisters have always called them Aunt Sue or Uncle Joe even though they aren't related, but we all love them dearly. I really love the fact that you all spread that love through the entire nation."

John just smiled and pulled him into a loving hug.

As a whole, the children in his school, from preschool through to the twelfth grade, behaved very well. When Jack commented to John about it, he responded, "They are two reasons. One, because their parents send them to school to learn, not misbehave, plus having your father's or mother's bow brought across your backside really hurts."

"And the other reason?" Jack asked.

John just smiled and touched his cheek. "They've been told by their parents about Little Spirit. Disappointing you isn't something they want to do. You're becoming their Little Spirit!"

Jack replied, "I can't wrap myself around this *Little Spirit* thing. It befuddles me. After all, I'm just doing my job. Just how do I discover what this name really means and why it was given to me?"

John answered, "Just be Jackson McIntire, and it'll become clear to you soon enough."

School continued to make progress. When he and Donna talked about just how well, he told her that it scared him a bit. Donna laughingly said, "What else would you expect, Dr. Obsessive Compulsive? Hmm?"

Things got difficult at times, especially when Hank and Jack went round and round about every detail. If Jack wanted an upgrade or repair of the school or its grounds, a battle always ensued. These mini battles proved interesting and sometimes unsettling. Mama Jena, the newly elected president of the school board, prevailed, and Hank, in the end, fixed the things that Jack requested. The school board mentioned in several meetings that the children seemed happy and well-adjusted to the new curriculum. Jack explained to the board that they were progressing very well in all areas.

Several weeks after school started, wild excitement broke out on the playground. The kindergarten class found a huge diamondback rattlesnake—most people hadn't ever seen one before. Even though terrified of snakes, Jack charged out to protect the children. Children in danger overrode any fear he had. Jack brought a broom and ordered them all to run into the school building, but they stayed and just stared at him.

"Run!" he shouted, but they stared wild-eyed first at Little Spirit, then the snake and back again. "*Anakipa!*" Jack shouted, and they turned and darted back to the school. Jack smacked the thing with the broom, but that just angered the snake more. It struck at Jack, and he flew backward. John caught him with one hand, and he shot the snake with the pistol in his other hand. Jack felt himself turn a little pale, and he gave his body an overall shake.

"I really hate snakes! I mean really, really hate them."

John nodded. "Jack, the kids are back inside the building and being checked carefully. We don't want to discover later that someone was bitten." When Jack realized the kids ran safely back into the building, he lost it for a second, and he teared up. But he regrouped. "I want a snake-proof fence and armed guards just in case this happens again, and I want a big monster shotgun, and I want . . ." John just pulled him in closer and shushed him. "I really hate snakes!"

"I remembered that." John chuckled but turned serious very quickly. "Little Spirit, you spoke the first Lakota word I've ever heard you say. And it was a good one!"

As the snakes-are-so-creepy feeling left him, Jack came back to life. "Let me go. I've a school to run."

Jena came running up with several others. Her eyes widened when she saw the broom and the large snake. "*Takos!* Are you okay? What were you thinking, taking on a rattler with only a broom? You could've been bitten or even killed." Then Jena looked again at the snake. "Oh, my God. That's the biggest rattler I've ever seen! Are you sure you weren't bitten?"

Before Jack could even respond, he saw the terror in John's eyes.

John started to tear at Jack's clothes, and Jack smacked John hard enough to make him stop. "*Enákiy!* I wasn't bitten! Stop, before you rip my clothes to shreds!" Jack snapped at John.

John flushed red, then whispered, "You're very important to me . . . as well as to this nation. I'll always react strongly when you're in danger."

Jack just melted as he looked into his warm, loving gaze. "Okay, time for me to go back to work before I do something embarrassing or stupid,"

Jena and all those with her laughed.

Chapter Six

John always seemed somewhere close by. Whenever Jack needed him, he'd suddenly appear at Jack's side. Sometimes Jack called his name, then turned around and ran right into him. At times it felt spooky to Jack that John just appeared like that. Jack told Jason, "I love to have John always close."

Jason's only comment was, "Now it's started. Walk gently, my brother."

The council decided to have big celebration on the Labor Day holiday. Every member of the tribe attended, from the smallest newborn to the oldest. The oldest, John's great-grandfather, Tȟuŋkášila Waŋblí, opened the celebration with a prayer. John told Jack that his name translated to Grandfather Golden Eagle, and in his prayer, he'd asked for the Great Father's blessings on the entire Lakota family.

As the day progressed, the old man told stories, and John translated for Jack. Grandfather remembered back to the old days when white people came and took away the children to be *educated*. In reality, they kidnapped them and forced them to learn the white man's ways. Tȟuŋkášila Waŋblí told them that the program didn't work so well.

"As soon as the children were old enough, most of them came back to the reservation, but so many forgot much of the Lakota ways. It took many years to bring them back to being fully Lakota again." Tȟuŋkášila Waŋblí then told John and Jack, "I'm so proud for our children to be educated here at home. Even though some didn't want a white man leading the school, the council made the best choice."

Jack was surprised at the old man's words. Jack leaned close to John. "Just how old is Great-Grandfather?"

John replied, "As far as anyone could figure it, Tȟuŋkášila Waŋblí's over one hundred years old, maybe as old as one hundred twenty years. He's lived so long that no one knows his exact birth year. But his memories go back several generations."

Jack saw that John's eyes sparkled when he spoke, the same way that his great-grandfather's eyes sparkled.

The old man took a great liking to Jack and insisted that he sit close to him. John kept close to interpret some of what Tȟuŋkášila Waŋblí said.

Tȟuŋkášila Waŋblí turned to Little Spirit and said, "*Ákhiyeuŋčheča. Uŋkíye nuphíŋ theȟíla John Núŋp Čhetáŋ.*"

John looked a bit shocked. Jack saw John's look and poignantly asked, "What exactly did he say?"

John turned very red. "He said we, meaning you and he, are alike. We both love John Two Hawks."

Little Spirit gaped at John for a split second, but that ended when Tȟuŋkášila Waŋblí patted his hand and smiled.

The two of them talked for a while longer, Tȟuŋkášila Waŋblí understood much more English than he could speak. But with John's help, the conversations were understood.

The stories he told intrigued Jack and kept him glued to his every word. John interpreted, but only when Jack looked to him for understanding.

After a time, John seemed to decide they needed to move on. He stood up, took Jack's hand, and pulled him up. Then he kissed his great-grandfather on the top of his head and said, "Time for dancing."

Tȟuŋkášila Waŋblí pulled on Little Spirits hand and said, "*Lakȟóta oyáte kiŋ lowáŋpi na wačhípi awáštelakapi.*"

John smiled broadly. "He said that all Lakota love to sing and dance."

Every able-bodied person danced for what seemed like hours and hours. Even old Thuŋkášila Waŋblí joined in. When it all ended, people had danced, sung, and eaten their fill, so now they were ready to go home. The goodbyes were said, and the council building emptied quickly.

Later, Jack told his brother all about the celebration and how he enjoyed every moment. He also mentioned that he was starting to fall even more for this wonderful gentle man named John Two Hawks. Jack confided in Jason, "People tell me it shows whenever the two of us are together, and I'm pretty sure that John feels that same." Jason laughed when Jack told him that John's mother had found a special place in his heart.

Jason said, "Jackson, you're way past falling in love. You're flat-out, full-fledged, puppy-dog in love."

Jack answered, "I know."

John walked Jack to and from school every day, and on weekends they explored the reservation. John explained much about life there on the reservation and how the land gave the nation life. If anyone gets expelled from here for any reason, it could be the death of them, because so much of every person's life is entwined with everyone else's life. The loneliness and isolation would be unbearable."

Jack nodded. "I can truly understand that."

Early one evening, Jack heard a knock on his door. When he opened it, to no surprise, there stood John Two Hawks. Only this time, John held flowers in his hand and was all dressed up. John handed Jack the flowers. "Little Spirit, will you go to dinner and a movie with me?"

Jack took the flowers and said, "Yes, but you'll have to give me a few minutes to get dressed." Jack quickly changed and joined John, and that was when he heard a mysterious hawk cry. It was the same cry he'd been hearing throughout the past few weeks.

Perplexed by the sound, Jack asked John, "Can you hear a hawk calling?"

"Sure, boy, you look great." And he quickly ushered Jack out of the house to start their date.

They dined at a very nice restaurant in a nearby town. Their meal turned out very romantic, with pleasant conversation. John smiled at Jack a lot and often reached out and took his hand. That had Jack smiling back.

Several people stopped and said hello to John, and John, in return, introduced them to Jack. One woman noticed that John was holding Jack's hand. "John, what's this all about?" she said and pointed to their clasped hands.

John smiled his killer smile and said, "MaryAnn, it's very nice seeing you again." That stopped the conversation, and the silence moved her away.

Jack winked at John. "Hmmm, and another smitten woman?"

John smiled but didn't respond.

After dinner, they went to see a movie call *Running Horse*, about Native Americans. In that small town, they showed only older movies. Jack watched for John's reactions. He laughed at some things that Jack saw no humor in and huffed at things Jack really believed to be authentically true. On the way home, they talked about those things and the difference between the real Lakota and the ones on the movie screen. When they got back home, John and Jack sat in John's truck and talked for a long time.

"I guess I'd better go inside," Jack said as he opened his door and stepped out. John walked him slowly to the door, John's hand on his waist.

John cleared his throat like he wanted to speak, but he looked down at his feet. Finally, John raised his head and looked into Jack's eyes. "Little Spirit, will you date only me, please?"

Jack relaxed and hoped it showed in his expression. "That's just the sweetest thing anyone's ever asked me." He paused for a moment and finally responded, "I will."

The whoop that John released probably awakened the entire reservation. Jack tried to put his hand over John's mouth and shush him, but he reached up too late. John ran off and whooped it up all the way back to his own house.

The next morning, bright and early, Jena Little Flower brought Jack a gift. She presented him with a beautifully carved wooden spoon. She told Jack, "You'll need this, *Takos*. This'll keep that wild stallion you've chosen in his place." They both laughed until they cried.

Jack hung it on the wall near the kitchen.

John eyeballed the giant spoon when he came over that evening. "What's that all about?"

"It's a gift your mother gave to me."

"Give it back, or better yet, throw it away," John said flatly but still eyed the spoon.

Jack moved over closer to John. He stood behind him and reached down and wrapped his arms around John's neck, touching their cheeks. "I could never do that, John, and you know it." Jack smiled and kissed John.

"Fine, I'll make sure it's firmly attached to the wall so it'll never fall off." He pulled Jack around into his lap and hugged him, but he still kept glancing back at the spoon from time to time.

Jack's body trembled. He was about to burst with amusement even as he tried very hard to keep it under control.

"Jackson, I know you're about to explode with laughter. I don't see this as funny."

That was the moment the pent-up laughter burst out, and

Jack laughed until tears rolled. At first, John only looked annoyed, but then Jack started to tickle his ribs, and the two of them laughed themselves silly.

True to his word, the next day, when Jack came home from school, John had bolted the spoon to the wall. "John, you're being silly about that spoon. Besides, if I ever move, I'll want to take it with me." John gave Jack a look that startled him, not quite a glare but close. Jack winked playfully back at him, curled into John's lap, and kissed him. John never made it home that evening.

Jack started it. After dinner, he cuddled and snuggled. John kissed him with such passion that Jack's body went from warm to flame-on-hot. Jack stood, took John's hand, and started pulling him up from the sofa. "Come with me," Jack invited.

John stood and followed him to the bedroom.

Slowly, John undressed as Jack sprawled out on the bed, and for the first time, Jack saw John's entire magnificent body.

His beautiful bronze skin and his very well-defined muscles started at his broad shoulders, then tapered down to his narrow waist and hips. John's body was smooth and hairless until you reached his thick, long, hard cock and heavy hanging balls. Everything was surprisingly hairy, considering John's hairlessness on the rest of his body. Jack desired him so much that he moaned.

John touched Jack's face and gently climbed onto the bed, and slowly started to undress him. He kissed every area he uncovered. "Jack, your magnificent body's so perfect and flawless. Every muscle can be felt under your alabaster skin, and may I say, for a man of your size, the man parts outdo themselves?"

John instinctively knew how to make Jack's body respond just as Jack could with John. They anticipated each other's bodies and what the other needed.

Passions exploded between them.

Later in the night, Jack murmured to John, "Never has a man made love to me like that." On and off all night, they continued making love, sharing so many emotions and passions. When the alarm clock went off, Jack mumbled, "This must be a joke." He felt totally exhausted.

John walked into the room with a hot cup of coffee and that beautiful smile that made Jack's body respond immediately. Jack was really falling hard for this man.

Later that day when he was alone, Jack called Jason and told him about John and their new closeness. Jason only wished him happiness.

John never really went back home much after that night.

Chapter Seven

October came on, and the days flew by. Everyone's hard work was paying off, and the new program was showing that the students were making progress. Little Spirit commented, "The people that developed the new program truly understood how these children learn."

Jack barely finished the evaluations of the teachers and got them sent to the state department in time to meet the deadline. He also needed to send a summary of student achievements and the data to back it up. Sometimes, Jack found it difficult to work with John around, as he constantly and easily distracted him. But somehow, he'd gotten it all done and turned it in on time, mostly thanks to Donna, who chased John out of the office whenever she caught him in it. She was like his guardian angel.

Just two weeks before Halloween, the crops were all harvested, and the animals that needed to be processed were either smoked, stored away in the tribal refrigerators, or frozen in the large freezers. Every person helped in their own way. Even Jack picked, chopped, or canned things. With the harvest completed, the reservation threw a big celebration.

The Council of Chiefs thanked the people for the efforts put forth, and several people sat in places of honor. Jack listened as each person stood as their contributions were proclaimed. Honored people humbly responded that they were only a part of the process.

Jack whispered to Jena about the people. "I'm awed at their humility and sense of community."

Jack suddenly heard his name called, and the surprise took his breath away.

John stood and told the gathering, "The school's progressed academically much faster than projected. All of this due to the fact Little Spirit came to us and gave us his all." It seemed like John went on forever, though, in reality, he only spoke for a minute. Jack felt himself blush. His pride in the progress the students made soon overrode any embarrassment.

Jack stood and responded, "You've said very kind words, thank you, but I'm only a very small part of why our school's successful. It's mostly thanks to the dedicated staff, to the parents, and the community, but more importantly, due to the hardworking children you've raised. Moving from the state-set curriculum to this program was a very progressive move. Well done, everyone." Jack sat down. He smiled proudly at the staff nearby as the room filled with applause.

When the applause died down, Jack breathed a sigh of relief.

John spoke again, "One more thing. Little Spirit?" Jack stood again but only because Jena gave him no choice as she elbowed him until he stood.

"Good, I've got your attention?"

Jack blushed and nodded.

John walked over to him. "Little Spirit, I want everyone to know, *Čhaŋtóčhignake.*" John paused, then translated, "I love you." Much to Jack's surprise, John had spoken the words out loud.

"I know what you said," Jack answered, and he saw the love that radiated from John. Jack's joyful tears worked their way to the surface. "I love you, too!" he said in return. John walked up to him, put his arm around Jack's shoulder, and pulled him in close.

They walked home from the gathering in silence. Finally,

John cleared his throat. "Jackson, I'm sorry if you weren't ready for everyone to know about us and that I put you on the spot. I guess I've so much love in my heart and soul for you that it makes my mouth run faster than my brain. Are you mad at me?"

Jack responded immediately. "What put that idea in your overly active brain? John, I think I've loved you from the first moment I saw you. I also realized there are no secrets in your world, that everything's family and community based. Čhaŋtóčhignake, John Two Hawks."

They walked through the front door, and as soon as it closed, John scooped him up. In an instant, they stepped behind a closed bedroom door. "How'd you do that? It's like you move the speed of light or something?" Jack asked.

"Warrior training."

That was good enough for Jack. Right now, he needed John.

As Halloween approached, Jack began to wonder how the reservation celebrated it or if they celebrated at all. He didn't want to offend anyone, so he casually asked John about it.

John told him, "It's not usually a day of celebration." He asked Little Spirit how his family celebrated it.

"We just have fun, not a real celebration at all, more like a big party. The kids and adults all dress up in costumes and go house to house trick or treating for candy, and then there's usually a party with activities and goodies for the kids. There are refreshments for both adults and children."

John looked at him puzzled and asked, "Why would your people do that?"

Jack looked at him, feeling perplexed.

John continued, "Why have the children go out and about begging for candy?"

Jack burst into laughter. "John, it isn't like that. People

prepare for the trick-or-treaters. Maybe it's a little similar to your tribal dances, and everyone dresses up for them, and there are always tons of food and things for the little ones. For our Halloween, everyone has fun and plays games, dances, and laughs. This Halloween stuff wasn't originally all fun and games. Many years ago, it was a nighttime event to ward off evil spirits, witches, demons, and that kind of stuff. After time passed, people no longer held those beliefs and most people understood that there weren't demons, witches, or evil spirits to ward off. They realized that it was still fun to dress up and pretend, so it all turned into a big party. That's about the best answer I can give you."

"Oh, my Little Spirit, all those things really do exist. You have so much to learn."

"Your Little Spirit?" Jack's expression softened.

A couple of days later, at the council meeting, there was an announcement that there would be a costume party.

Jack talked with John about it. "I'm quite sure this is totally for my benefit. I'm guessing you arranged it all so I won't miss home so much." John smiled his make-your-knees-weak smile and said nothing. "But how are you going to put this all together with such short notice?"

"Little Spirit, we live on a reservation, not another planet. The party part's easy. We can throw that together in no time. The costume part may be a little more difficult, but everyone'll manage and have fun doing it. There are plenty of costumes from the high school plays, and others'll just make due."

The event proved entertaining and fun. From the oldest to the youngest, everyone dressed up. Jack decided to be a pirate. He thought he looked pretty good, too. Jack made John surprise him with his costume. In turn, he'd surprised John.

Jack walked to the Council Hall, and along the way, he met

ghosts and ghouls and witches, monsters, and all kinds of famous people. Everyone laughed and complimented each other's costumes.

Then Jack entered the hall, and there stood John. Jack stopped awestruck as he stared at that beautiful man, John, dressed as a prince, a Native American Prince Charming for sure. What a prince he made.

"Close your mouth. You're drooling." Donna popped Jack's mouth shut as she walked by him.

Jack walked straight into John's arms.

John asked, "She's dressed as what?" He nodded toward Donna.

Jack quietly guessed, "Maybe as a diesel dyke biker?"

"Ha! I think you're right. I feel so stupid," John said, chuckling.

"Well, you look incredibly hot. But if I were you, I wouldn't get too turned on in that costume. As huge as you are, the world would know." Jack tickled him.

John pushed him back to look him in the face. "You think I'm huge?"

"Ah, yeeeah!" Jack gave him that what-a-stupid-question look.

Jena appeared dressed as the Queen of Hearts, followed closely by Thomas as the King of Hearts. They walked up and greeted John, Jack, and everyone standing around them. They all went to the refreshment table where they chatted and sipped punch. They noticed when Kitten came in as Dorothy with ruby slippers and all. And her husband, *Mr. I Coach*, entered as the Cowardly Lion.

John looked at Little Spirit and said, "How appropriate!"

Jack hadn't noticed that Hank walked through the doors as a penguin. But when John saw him, he spat punch everywhere. Jack quickly turned to see what had choked him. There stood a gigantic penguin. Laughter filled the room. Hank cringed and started to back out, but he soon realized the source of entertainment really wasn't him, but rather the fact that when John sprayed out punch, the bulk of it sprayed his mother, the Queen of Hearts, and she just flipped out.

John realized what he'd done. "I'm really sorry, Ma! It was an accident!" Jack watched as John instantly took off with the Queen of Hearts in hot pursuit. John returned a little sweaty and winded. "She didn't catch me." He panted.

"Yet." Jack heard Jena from behind them.

Jack stepped in and saved poor John. "Jena, it was an accident, and this is a party. Please, can you just kill him later?" She squinted her eyes and pointed her finger menacingly at John, but she then joined the laughter along with her husband and the others standing around.

"Thanks, I think," John said, but he still looked around wildly, anticipating a strike at any moment from his mother.

The party turned out to be so much fun. People laughed, danced, and mingled everywhere in the hall. Jack watched and saw that almost everyone enjoyed themselves a great deal.

When the ball finally finished, John and Jack walked home. John was very quiet, but Jack continued to prattle on and on about the ball.

As they undressed, Jack finally asked John, "You had a good time, didn't you?"

"It was fun." John sounded flat.

"So, what do you think you'll dress up as next year?" Jack asked.

"As me! Little Spirit, I'm a chief of the Lakota. Isn't that enough for you? Are you so ashamed of me being Native America that you'd have to dress me up to look different?"

Jack felt shocked and then hurt. "First of all, this was not my idea, plus so you know, John, when I saw you dressed up today, I didn't see the storybook prince, I saw a Native

American prince, and that's how I saw everyone, no matter what costume they had on. Except for Hank, I saw an honest-to-goodness penguin."

Jack laughed a little, and John gave a weak smile. "John, I know you did this for me, and it was wonderful that you wanted me to feel a little more like I was at home. However, John, we never have to do anything like that again. If the only way you can feel comfortable is by having everything stay the way it was before I came, then I'll try to do that."

Jack paused, looked at John, and then continued, "John, while you've had to readjust your life some for me, I want you to think about everything I had to adjust in my life to be here to be part of your life. I could've just come and set the school up, and it would've been successful, but I've tried to learn everything I could about your people, your customs, your dietary patterns, the ins and outs of how to address each person. Moreover, I'm trying to learn your native tongue, which is a very complicated language and very difficult to learn. I know we have our differences, but I was pretty sure they were so minuscule that we'd never be bothered by them, I was wrong, and I'm sorry I misread you. John, I love you, but right now, I need to be alone to think about all this."

John reached for him, but Jack stepped back. Part of Jack was hurt, and part of him felt stupid.

"Please go home, John. I really need to think about how I could've been so carelessly wrong." Jack saw the extreme sadness in John's eyes, but he still needed John to go. Jack wanted some distance to think about their situation and how he'd misread the entire relationship.

Jack had woken a dozen times and reached for John, but he'd touched no one. Even though Jack felt John's touch and smelled his scent in the room, the room remained empty when he turned on the light to check. At three in the morning, he wasn't able to sleep. He just lay awake and listened to some damn hawk that called for his mate over and over again. It sounded mournful and painful to hear.

Unable to lie in bed anymore, he got up. He went to the bathroom and peed. Then he took a look at himself in the mirror and saw his swollen, tired eyes. What a scary sight to behold. Jack hoped the cold water he splashed on his face would bring down the swelling. He went into the kitchen and made the first cup of coffee he'd made in weeks. John always made perfect coffee.

Jack sat down at the kitchen table to think. He took a pen and paper and started a list of the best things for him to do. On the left side of the paper, he wrote all the reasons he needed to return home to his parents. The right side listed all the things he loved about John and this place and the reasons for him to stay. But, despite the long list on the right, Jack wasn't sure what to do.

Bang! Bang! Bang!

Four AM, and someone was banging at his door. As he reached for the knob, he heard Jena, "I know you're awake and can hear me. Open this door!" she demanded.

When he opened it, his heart sank. There stood a much disheveled John. He looked as though he had gotten less sleep than Jack. Jena and Thomas shoved John at Jack, and then they stepped into Jack's house. John's sad eyes spoke volumes. Jena took one look at Jack and then moved her glare to John. "Did you strike that precious boy?"

John stepped back in horror at her accusation. "Ma! Of course, I didn't!"

"Look at him. You've done something to him!" Thomas stated.

Jack intervened, "He spoke the truth about how he felt."

Jena sounded irritated, and at the end of her patience. "Well, something's very wrong here, and John prowled around outside all night long."

"Jena, that's more than enough." Thomas sounded curt and final. Jena went silent. "Son, what's this about?" He expected an answer.

"Dad, he's going to leave, and it's all my fault. I let pride in myself and being Lakota get in the way of my love for him. I only saw that I was going to have to change, and I didn't like it. I never even thought how much Little Spirit had already changed and will have yet to change, just because he loves me. I was a damn fool, and I'm sorry."

The pain in John's words made Jack take a step toward him.

"Why are you telling me this? Tell him, you idiot!" Chief Thomas barked.

Jena looked John. "What on earth's wrong with you? You've—"

Chief Thomas raised his hand. "We'll let them work this out on their own. Let's go, Jena."

She shot a glass-cutting glare that was focused entirely on John, and he flinched as she walked by. They closed the door behind them.

"Are you really planning on leaving?" John's voice was shaky.

Jack just shrugged.

"Can I go with you, if you go?" John's voice trembled with emotion.

Jack stood in total confusion. "John, you can't leave our people. They need you." Jack looked him straight in the eye.

"You said *our* people. Did you mean it, or was it a slip of the tongue?"

Jack slowly responded, "These are my people. You all are part of my family, just as are my parents and family back on the farm. I've room in my heart for them all and an understanding that each one's different and with different needs."

"Jackson, stay with me. Please, stay with me.

Čhaŋtóčhignake."

There was sorrow in John's voice as he pleaded for Jack to stay. This display of vulnerability was something John had never showed Jack before. Jack reached for him, and John pulled him into his arms.

"What made you change your mind?" Jack asked, stepping back.

"Change my mind? Never for one second did I ever want you to leave me. I wandered around, searching my mind and soul. I realized two things. First, that I loved you more than life itself and that you're the half of my soul that was missing all these years. And two, I finally understand the giant steps you took to come here and then had to adapt so you could live here with me. And that I'd done nearly nothing to reciprocate, and I'm so sorry. I'm such an idiot, but I'm the idiot that loves you beyond the reach of the stars." He drew a very shaky breath and looked at Jack with such sorrowful but love-filled eyes. "Please, Little Spirit, stay with me."

Jack didn't leave him hanging anymore. He threw himself into John's arms, and Jack caught him around his neck. John stumbled back but caught Jack by the waist. Amazingly, John quickly righted himself, got his footing, and carried Jack back to their bedroom. The rest of that day was filled with their passion for each other.

That next morning, Jack called Donna to tell her he wouldn't be in, and took a sick day. He told her she was in charge. Donna laughed and said, "I didn't know doing what you two are doing made people sick." She was still laughing when she hung up. God help the person that messed up under her watch.

The next incredible twenty-four hours mended all misunderstandings.

Later they lay in bed and talked about this and that. Then

John asked, "Jack?"

"Yes, my chief." Jack was playful and teasing.

"Knock that crap off. Do your parents know we're living together?" That question caught Jack off guard. Just one sheepish glance from Jack, and he let John know that he hadn't told them.

"Why are you asking me that?" Jack came across so sweetly.

Not fooled, John asked again, "Well, do they?"

Jack tried to avoid answering, but John shook his head and redirected him to answer, which left him no choice. "Not exactly, you see, John, my parents won't approve of us living together."

"They approve of you being gay but not you living as a gay man?"

"No, that's not it. It doesn't matter to my parents if their kids are gay or straight, but living together without a formal marriage ceremony isn't acceptable."

John freaked out. "They're going to hate me even before they get to meet me! I've got to move out!" John pounced on Jack. "You should've told me this major detail long ago." John held Jack down playfully but firmly.

"I promise to tell them," Jack said through giggles.

"Okay . . . when?"

"Soon, John, I promise."

"Here, I'll get your phone, and you can tell them now." John got up to get Jack's phone, but Jack shot off to the bathroom. When John returned, he tried the bathroom door, it was locked, so he called to Jack, "You can't hide in there forever."

Jack yelled back, "Sorry, I can't hear you. I'm in the shower."

John shouted back, "That isn't going to work for long."

That evening, Jack confided in Jason about the fact he hadn't told their parents about his and John's living arrangements. "Our folks are going to blow a gasket. Better you than me." Jason laughed. No laughter came from Jack.

CHAPTER EIGHT

November was already underway when Jack's mom and dad called him. They invited John to come with him for Thanksgiving. Jack had promised long ago to go to the farm for the holiday, but he seriously doubted that John would come. Jack knew that his mom, Melissa, never took no for an answer.

"Now, you ask that young man of yours, and you'd better show up with him, and I mean it."

"I'll ask him, Mom, but I'm sure John has other obligations." He pretty much figured John wanted to stay there on the reservation with his family.

Jack's mom wanted none of that, "Ask him!"

Jack hung up and found John in the kitchen where he'd started making supper. "John, my parents have asked me to invite you to come to Thanksgiving and you could meet the family."

"Sure. When do we leave?" John responded simply. He continued to cook supper, but it seemed for a second that he'd smiled at Jack.

That totally surprised Jack.

"Jack, you're doing that fish mouth thing again." He drew a circle in front of Jack's mouth to make his point.

"You want to come with me and meet my entire family?"

"Little Spirit, I want them to like me before we get married—again with the fish mouth thing." John pulled him in for a huge hug. Jack hugged back but still felt like a deer caught in someone's headlights.

"You're always full of surprises, and I never know what to expect," Jack mumbled into John's chest.

Everyone in Jack's family came home for Thanksgiving except for Jack's brother Jason. He worked in the diplomatic corps in South Africa and said he'd used all his vacation days in Europe.

Jack and John barely got out of the car when most of family came out to meet them with smiles and handshakes. Jack's dad, Andy McIntire, drew him into a big bear hug, and his mom hugged his neck and kissed him. They warmly welcomed John into their home.

They moved into the house for family introductions. Jack's oldest sibling, Iris, acted a little snotty at first, but Jack's mom quickly put that attitude of hers in check. "Iris, behave or go home."

Iris always bossed people around and stuck her nose in everyone's business. In spite of that, her big heart always showed itself. Her husband of fifteen some years, Roger, and her three girls introduced themselves. Her youngest, Joe-Joe, hid behind his father, but he finally got the courage to ask John, "Are you real?"

John smiled, then squatted down to be on Joe-Joe's level and answered, "Yep."

Joe-Joe beamed at John. "Great!"

When John stood up Iris's youngest girl, Mimi, reached up to be picked up, and John complied. She ran her fingers through his hair and kissed his nose. John hugged her close and kissed her nose, too. She squirmed to get down and ran off to find something to else entertain her.

Next in line was Robert, aka Bert, and his wife Emmie. He ran the farm with his twin brother, Timmy, and his wife, Carmi, and of course, all under the supervision of their dad, Andy. They'd both married very young and produced five kids apiece—everyone teased them about the twin competition between them.

Peter, next in line, born deaf, signed his hello, and much to Jack's utter surprise, John signed back and continued to sign the rest of the introductions. Peter, a professor, taught at Gallaudet University, with a doctorate in psychology.

Mary Rose and her brood of four boys came next. Her husband, Leo, the local veterinarian, got called out on an emergency that morning.

Cassie, aka Sister Mary Lucille, smiled and hugged John. Her brother, Father Michael, shook John's hand and welcomed him.

Jenny said hello as she was next, and she introduced her husband, Phil, and two boys and three foster kids, all darling little girls.

Helen came next with her two boys and said hello. Jack told John earlier that she lost her husband, Dan, five years ago in a massive fire at the downtown warehouse. Dan was a fireman.

Nick came next—a total computer nerd—with his partner, Alex.

That only left Jason, Jack's best friend and closest sibling, who'd stayed in South Africa.

Everyone chatted and asked questions. John signed for Peter and answered every question so honestly that Jack's family got a bit taken aback. Iris suddenly decided she liked John and stepped in and took over as interpreter for Jack's brother.

The little guys attacked John with questions. "Do you have a war bonnet? How come you don't have paint on your face?" Little Tommy asked wide-eyed. "Have you ever scalped anyone?" Jack leaped up and covered his nephew's mouth but not in time.

"Yes, I have a chief's ceremonial headdress, and yes, I do put on paint, but only when it's appropriate, such as at huge dances and ceremonial gatherings. And, no, little guy, I've never scalped anyone." John wrinkled his nose and said, "That's kinda creepy, don't you think?" Everyone nodded in agreement.

The little ones all gathered in close, mesmerized by John's stories. He told factual and sometimes surprising stories of his culture and history, and they all just listened intently. The stories included those of his people long ago when they roamed as warriors of the plains and stories of how the settlers tried to have them wiped out with disease, then took away their children. Jack's mother and sisters cried. Jack tried not to, but he couldn't help it.

John pulled Jack in and hugged him close. "That's why I love you so much, Little Spirit." John then told of how Jack took out Hank and how he stood so bravely before the Tribal Council. He also told them, "It was that day I fell head over heels for Jack."

Jack said shyly. "Me, too."

Then one of the little guys asked John, "How do Injuns celebrated Thanksgiving?"

Jack cringed and watched John's reaction. With the dignity of a king, John smiled and pulled that little guy into his lap and told them about Native American customs. John explained, "On our reservation, Thanksgiving's called *Wophila Anpetu* and isn't the same as here at your grandparents' house. Back at home, my people gather to give thanks for the harvest and have the holy men and women bless all of the children born that year. Then they bless all of the food we harvested and preserved. But Thanksgiving's an everyday occurrence to the Lakota. So rather than having one day to be thankful for, our people try and be thankful for what we have every day."

John had brought some special foods with him for everyone to sample. Special marinated venison, buffalo steaks, and smoked pheasant, as well as very specially prepared bread and pudding-like dessert made from prairie berries. Jack helped John heat up, cook, and prepare the food. Then they laid out the entire spread. The family stared in awe at the large amount of food. Jack's father broke the ice and tried a little bit of everything. The look of pure pleasure on his face enticed everyone to get some before it all disappeared. Jack's family engulfed the entire meal, and John smiled with pride.

John usually never strayed far from Jack, but now Jack needed to hunt for John. When Jack found him, he wrapped his arms around John's waist and hugged him. John took Jack's face. "Jack, I'm proud to be your boyfriend, and thanks for not being afraid to show your family that you love me."

That evening, John got quite a surprise. He found out that he'd be sleeping on the other side of the house, far away from Jack.

"No unmarried cohabitation." That was a direct quote from Jack's dad.

John shot Jack a look. Jack understood he was not happy, but he never threw Jack under the wagon. When John finally cornered Jack, he asked, "You didn't tell them yet, did you? You're a little chicken shit."

"No. Are you mad at me?"

"I should be, I should be furious, but I can't be. But you'll tell them before they come for Christmas! Promise me!" John's face showed total seriousness, and Jack promised to clear this up long before that.

That night after everything settled down and quiet prevailed, John slipped into Jack's bed. Jack never even heard him open or close the door. He never saw any light from the hallway. He'd been lying awake and thinking about how much he missed John. John just appeared, and Little Spirit whispered, "My dad will cut your balls off if he catches you here."

"In that case, I better make sure he doesn't catch me then, huh," he whispered into Jack's neck.

At nearly seven AM, Jack's mom knocked on the bedroom door and opened it, "Get up!" Panic set in as Jack's eyes searched for John. "Your boyfriend, sweet man that he is, has been up for a couple of hours and made the best coffee I've ever had. Out of bed, slacker!"

"Okay, okay, I'm awake. Now step out, please."

"Why?" she asked innocently.

Jack rolled his eyes—she just had to ask. "Mom, you know mornings aren't good for me, and I sleep naked. Get out before I snap your head off! I'm getting up now. I mean this second."

Melissa quickly left.

First breakfast, then church, and as soon as they arrived home, Thanksgiving dinner preparations started. The family got busy with the Thanksgiving dinner. Melissa assigned everyone a task to do. The feast included it all, turkeys and all the trimmings, potatoes, both sweet and white, bean casseroles, pies, cranberries, and freshly baked bread.

The children set the table while the adults brought in the food. Everyone was seated.

Andy said the blessing, then began the traditional "I'm thankful for . . ." Andy was usually pretty stoic, but this time he teared up when he talked about the fact that most of his family gathered there but not all and how he hoped next year they'd all be there His words touched everyone. Sniffles and coughs to cover emotions came from those around the table.

Everyone shared what he or she was thankful for. Some announced a new baby or other exciting news. Jack was next to last. "I'm thankful for finding the wonderful job I have, and in doing that, I also got to meet John. I never knew what love was until he came into my life." His voice filled the room with emotion, so he stopped before he got too emotional.

John's turn came next. He looked at Jack, then the entire McIntire family. "Oh, I guess it's my turn. I'm thankful for the opportunity to share this meal, and that I've had time with this wonderful family I feel so much a part of. But now the hardest part . . ." The room filled with an awkward silence that seemed to last forever, causing everyone to look at John. John turned, pushed his chair back, and got down on one knee. He then took Jack's hand and met his surprised gaze. John swallowed hard. "Little Spirit, will you marry me?" The entire room froze.

"What did you say?" a very surprised Jack asked, sure he misunderstood him.

"Jackson Lee McIntire, will you marry me?" John said with a steady, clear voice. Every eye in the room went from John to Jack and back again.

Jack gaped, his mouth moved, but nothing came out for a second. He then sat up straighter, met John's loving gaze, and said, "Yes, John Two Hawks, I'll marry you."

John jumped up and pulled him into his arms. The room exploded with people cheering and clapping. Jack's mom and dad rushed them and hugged and kissed them both. The entire family embraced and congratulated the two of them. The news started to settle into Jack's brain, and the family returned back into their dinners, and they all ate, shared, talked, and gossiped.

After the meal resumed, Melissa said, "Have you thought about a date? I'll have to get the farm ready for a wedding, and I'll need some time."

John stilled for a second. "I'm so sorry to have to say this, Mr. and Mrs. McIntire. Oops, I mean Andy and Melissa, but

I'm a chief of my people. I must marry on the reservation in the ceremonial wedding area. It isn't optional."

Everyone started shouting with excitement about going to the reservation or that Jack might not marry at the place that every one of his family members got married before him. Jack's father silenced the room with just one hand clap. He then settled the entire matter. "You all will stop. There'll be no further discussion. We'll respect John's traditions."

John lit up like a kid getting his first puppy. "Thanks for understanding," he said back to Jack's dad.

Jack cleared his throat. "Do I have any say in this issue at all?"

His mom, dad, and John all responded precisely at the same time, "No."

The meal continued.

During a lull, Jack stated, "John, if it's all right with you, I'd like to be married in the spring when the prairie flowers are in bloom."

"You expect me to wait until then?" John teased. It was at that moment that Jack's phone rang. The caller ID showed John's mother. Jack just handed it to John, who said hello, then put it on speakerphone.

Nosey Jena got right to the point. "So, John, did you ask?"

"Ya, Ma, I did, and he said yes." There must've been a dozen other people on the other end that whooped it up and celebrated their news.

"Shhhhhh. Shush. When will it be?" Jena asked, but not where.

"Ma, it'll be when the prairie flowers bloom in the spring, around May fifteenth." He looked at Jack for approval, and he nodded yes.

"Little Spirit's making you wait that long, is he?" She then laughed, and Jack and John heard laughter in the background and around the table.

So without so much as a word from Jack or John, their mothers finalized their wedding plans.

At about four in the afternoon the next day, the men all walked back into the house from chores. They all wanted some coffee or hot chocolate. A car shot down the driveway. No one recognized it, but as soon as it stopped and the person got out, the entire McIntire clan knew him.

Jack reddened, and his temper rose. "Damn! It's Richard Carl Dyson. What the fuck! He's got a hell of a lot of nerve to show up here."

Jack's dad said it all when he shouted out to Richard. "We don't allow shit to accumulate here on the farm, so get the hell off my land!"

"I'm here to see Jack, old man, so butt out," Richard said rudely to Andy.

Every man in the family took a step forward. Jack shook his head and said, "Some things never change. Once an idiot, always an idiot. What do you want?" Jack demanded.

"I need to talk with you, to apologize, but I'd like to do it in private. Can we go somewhere?"

Jack felt John's protective hand on his shoulder. Jack smiled. "I got this," Jack said, stepped down the stairs, and walked out to Rick.

"Say what you've got to say and go."

"I knew you still loved me. I could tell by the way you're looking at me. I just knew you couldn't stay mad at me. You love me too much."

Jack's emotions soured. He snapped back, "Love you? Eew. I despise everything about you! Now you've said your piece, so go."

Jack turned to walk away, and Richard grabbed his arm. He spun Jack around, took his other arm, and started to shake him. "You'll come back to me, and right now!" Richard sounded and looked crazed.

Instantly, John appeared, and Richard lay on the ground with a bloody face. "Keep your filthy hands off my fiancée, you low-life piece of weasel shit," John shouted at the man.

Jack had never seen John like this before. His expression showed absolute fury, and Jack saw the black rage in his eyes. He looked ready to kill.

John picked up Jack and carried him to Jack's father. "Keep him here and safe." Jack's father nodded in acknowledgment. John turned and flew back to Richard, who scrambled to get into his car.

John grabbed him and literally threw him into the car. "Never do I want to see your face again." John's anger showed all over his face, his words spewed out like arrows being shot, and Richard's body responded as if it was happening.

Richard nodded and started his car.

As he backed out, he rolled down the window and shouted, "Who'd want you now after you've been with that filthy injun!" Some of the men on the porch charged the car. He screamed, "Oh, shit!" Rick twirled his vehicle around and shot off the farm going zero to ninety.

John returned to the porch and immediately reached for Jack and pulled him in close. "Little Spirit, are you all right?" John reverted back to his tender and loving self.

"Yes, but you didn't have to intervene. I could've handled him all by myself, but, oh, no . . . you just had to warrior all up, didn't you? And carry me up to my father for protection? Come on. You couldn't control yourself, could you?" Jack ruffled up like a little banty rooster as he huffed at John.

John only smiled his smile, which made Jack's knees weak. "Little Spirit, you're my promised one, my soul mate. No one will ever be able to show hostility toward you without me reacting. Every time someone does, I'll intervene. After all, hawks mate for life, and both would sacrifice themselves to save their mate." John drew him into his embrace.

The men all reenacted the incident scene by scene for Jack's mother, sisters, sisters-in-law, and the kids. They loved the story. Bert's youngest, Andrew Wyatt, chirped in, "You should've scalped him!" Every person gasped and turned to John, and to his credit, John burst into the most contagious laugh and agreed. He then picked up Andrew Wyatt and did a victory war dance.

Jack whispered to his mother, "Mom, I'm so happy that everyone loves John."

"Honey, he's good and loving man, just like you, so it's natural for us to love him." She hugged her son.

Later, Jack looked out of the window and watched his brothers as they walked around and seemed to look for something in the snow. He threw on his jacket and went out to help.

"Hey, you guys, what's up?" he shouted from the porch.

"Jack com-mere," Bert shouted back.

"So, what's up?" Jack asked as he joined them.

"Jack, we all saw John go after Rick. It was so great seeing that asshole get his comeuppance. I swear to you, it was like John just flew to you, and there are no footprints."

"I did, well, sort of." John put his arms suddenly around Jack's waist, pulling him in close.

"John, there're no footprints of you going all the way to where Rick and Jack stood."

Bert's raised eyebrow and wide-opened eyes expressed his concern and bewilderment.

"Moccasins and Lakota warrior training helped to keep me walking on top of the snow." John jokingly said, "What, did you think, I'd flown?" Everyone burst into laughter. Jack looked at John, and John winked at him. John had charmed everyone, just like he'd charmed Jack.

Jack leaned into him and said, "I'm glad you do. Love you, too." The men all looked at Jack like he was nuts. Jack swore to God he heard him say *I love you* first. The men all looked at the two of them.

John smiled at the group and said, "Sometimes the words can be unspoken."

The rest of the time with the family turned out just perfect. Jack found it hard to say goodbye, but nothing could've stopped him from going home with John.

CHAPTER NINE

Jack's first winter in the northern plains proved very hard. The weather turned deadly cold, and snow accumulated more and more nearly every day. On top of all that, the wind blew endlessly. From Thanksgiving weekend until just days before Christmas, it never got above minus fifteen, and blizzard after blizzard hit them. They had over six feet of snow. John said one very bitterly cold evening, "Better bring the brass monkeys in tonight." Jack always looked confused when he said that.

Finally, Jack asked, "What on earth do you mean?"

"Have you never heard *it is cold enough to freeze the balls off a brass monkey*?" John asked.

"No, but I get the meaning."

"I would hope so, seeing as you have *D.R.* in front of your name." John often laughed heartily at his own jokes, but just as often, Jack never cracked even a smile.

Every able-bodied person bundled up and shoveled or plowed snow. Even the kids helped. They frequently needed to go inside to get warm, then back outside to shovel some more. Snowplows and tractors continuously ran to keep roads as open as possible.

Early back when the snow started, Jack had told John, "When it gets below zero, the snow will stop."

John smiled, "Maybe where you lived, but not around here."

Jack learned to start and ride a snowmobile and even ski behind it. John, never far from his side, tried to always catch him before he fell or picked him up if he did fall.

The snow became impossible, and Jack no longer used his car. "John, even the school buses are having a hard time with this snow, and they've got four-wheel drive and chains on the tires."

"Don't worry, we'll get through this. We're used to this kind of winter."

Jack learned a few things about walking on snow-packed roads and sidewalks. First, never wear dress shoes—wear snow boots. Second, when you fell, you instinctively looked around to see who saw you, not if you had any injuries. The third thing, when you fell, everyone asked, "Are you okay? Did you hurt yourself?"

Jack told John, "That's such a stupid question, because it always hurts when you hit the ground at the speed of light. Even if there were no physical injuries, the humiliation alone proves painful."

John just burst into laughter. "It's so true. The humiliation's the worst part."

Finally, Jack learned that when people watched anyone else slip and fall on the icy snow, it made them laugh, including him. When Donna slipped and fell in front of the school, Jack thought he'd explode as he tried to contain his amusement. But Donna informed everyone around, "Laugh, and I'll make you all eat yellow snow." Not one person so much as snickered. They all knew she'd follow through.

John got up early every morning and made coffee and breakfast, and of course, he nearly had to force Jack to eat something. Although he still wasn't a morning person and he still snapped at anything that moved, Jack started to enjoy his breakfast time with John. Every morning after breakfast, John started up the snowmobile and drove them both to school, as the snow was now so damn deep that walking had become nearly impossible. Sometimes several dozen snowmobiles with sleds attached were parked outside the building. Inside the school's front door, blankets and animal skins were piled to warm up for the ride home.

Children rarely missed a day of school. Jack discovered that perfect attendance ran at ninety-seven percent for all the students. So when three of the students remained out of school for four days in a row with no word of why, Jack became very concerned. Donna tried to call the family, but to no avail. Phone service appeared out in some areas.

Jack decided to go find out what had kept the children out of school. He drove the snowmobile out to their home. He traveled without many landmarks to follow and all around was nothing but white. By some miracle, he found his way to the family's home. All three of the children had caught terrible colds. Even so, excitement filled the room that their Little Spirit came to their house and checked on them. Jack called Jena. He needed her know about the sickness and that the mother needed medical supplies and food.

Jena picked up after only one ring. "*Takos*! Where are you? John's so worried, and he's about to get the entire community out looking for you!" She sounded concerned.

Jack quickly explained his location and why he went there.

"You of all people should've figured out that you never travel alone out on the snow-covered prairie, especially if you don't know and understand the lay of the land. John's heading out now to get you. You need to wait until he gets there, okay?"

Jack hated to be a burden. "Jena, I'll just head out and meet him halfway."

Jack hung up and put his phone away. He started his machine and took off. The engine drowned out Jena's attempts to call and stop him. Several miles out from the family's home, Jack's snowmobile just died. "Shit and damn!" Jack said as he saw the gas gauge needle was on *E*. He now needed to walk nearly a mile back to the school.

Jack knew that people died in North Dakota's forever unforgiving weather. The wind started to pick up as Jack walked, and at times, he would break through the snow and would have to pull his legs out. Jack realized he'd made a mistake when the wind started to cover the snowmobile tracks that brought him out here. He made the good decision to turn back and get to the snowmobile and wait for help. Jack luckily saw it off in the distance. It was the wisest decision.

John was nearly frantic when he reached the sick children's house. The children's mother told him that Jack took off a half-hour ago. John pulled out his phone and called Jack.

"John, I think I'm in trouble. I'm so cold," Jack said in a barely audible voice. John knew his Little Spirit needed immediate help.

"Jack, tell me if you hear a hawk calling. Jack! Can you hear me? Jack!" Panic started to rise in John, but he had to concentrate.

"I hear that hawk. *Čhaŋtóčhignake,*" Jack whispered.

John focused all his attention on those words, and in an instant, he knew where to find that little man he loved so much.

John quickly called his mother so she could spread the word. Jena ran through the snow to sound the alarm. John would have a sound to follow home, as it'd already turned dark. The snow and wind picked up even more. John flew over the snow on the snowmobile, guided by his inner spirit and his love for Jack. He found Little Spirit clinging to the snowmobile. He was alive, but just barely. John unzipped his heavy jacket, pulled Jack into it, and zipped it back up as best he could.

He took off full speed ahead and followed the alarm sound.

Their ride home took ten minutes. John tried to keep Little Spirit as warm as he could. The snowmobile flew into the schoolyard, and it left a fantail of snow in its wake. There were a dozen people waiting to help.

A couple of the men helped John off the machine and helped both Jack and him into the building. People inside were well prepared and took over. They peeled Jack away from John even though he protested. One group worked on Jack, and the other on John.

"No, not me, I'm fine, save my Little Spirit," John's raspy voice said over and over again. The people heeded nothing and just worked on them both.

Then John heard the sound he so desperately needed hear, his Little Spirit's weak voice. "I'm so cold. Where's John? Is John safe?"

John pushed everyone aside and walked to Little Spirit. "I'm here, and we're safe."

Everyone remained silent. John slid next to Jack and pulled him close. Heated blankets engulfed them, and sleep overtook them both.

John awoke in his bed, and he panicked until his reach found Little Spirit. He vaguely remembered that they'd been moved home. "Jack, honey, are you okay?" John whispered.

"He probably can't hear you, as Doc gave him a nice dose of pain medication." John's mother, Jena, spoke softly. "He suffered some minor frostbite on his toes and fingers. He'll be one hundred percent okay, but as you know, it can be painful coming back from frostbite, even minor frostbite. Are you okay, my son?" Jena lovingly brushed the hair from his face.

"Ma." John's voice was filled with the emotion he was feeling. "I nearly lost him today."

"I know, son."

"Ma, it would've killed me. Remember when you and Dad

told me that one day I'd find that person that'd fill the part of my soul that I felt was missing?" Teary-eyed, Jena nodded. "Ma, he's it. He's my every reason for existing. I can't live without him."

She lovingly stroked his cheek. "Before Little Spirit came, your father and I worried about whether you would ever find someone. We knew you were very lonely. Being gay isn't easy anywhere you live, but here it can be very hard. Some will never be accepting, and others won't care. We watched as you found yourself and grew in spirit, body, and soul into the proud man you've become. Your happiness has filled the air since that day that boy appeared. We all saw the change in you and how your inner self came out. We know that you love him, son. Your father and I, well, actually most of the community, couldn't be happier for you."

"Ma, how will I ever keep him safe? I want to lock him up in our home and keep him there, safe from harm," John said as he looked at Jack, then his mother.

"Son, he's Little Spirit. You've got to let his spirit soar. If you try and restrain him, he'll fight back. If you block his ability to grow and to find his own way, you'll break his spirit, and then he'll wither and disappear because he wouldn't be Little Spirit anymore." Jena again smiled, patted his hand, and left.

John checked to be sure Little Spirit was warm, but discovered that he was awake. John wrapped his arms around Jack and held on tight. "Listen to me, Little Spirit. You're the best part of my life, so you need to take things to heart when people tell you it isn't in your best interest to do something. You often run off half-cocked without seeing what consequences there could be." John was sincere.

"We can talk about this, or we could be making love," Jack whispered in John's ear. The discussion ended instantly.

Jack called a school board meeting, and they decided, with the weather predicted to get worse, that the school should be closed until the new year. The children were thrilled. It was a very good decision on the board's part.

"I'm sorry that I was so careless driving alone in the snow," Jack told John when they got home.

"Little Spirit, my hawk will always watch over you and protect you."

"Just what do you mean by your hawk? John, is there more to you than I know? I've heard you speak of your hawk several times, and I thought it was probably an animal spirit that the holy person chose for you."

"No." It was the only word John spoke. They walked up the shoveled walkway in complete silence until they reached the door.

"John? Talk to me. This silence worries me."

John pulled him inside and took his coat. He hung it up along with his own and led him into the living room. Jack sat as John built a fire. Then John joined him on the davenport. "Little Spirit, I've something I need to tell you. It may be very hard for you to believe, or maybe better, hard for you to understand. Please, just listen, and when I'm finished, you can ask me anything, okay?"

"John, you're making me nervous. Just say what you've got to say. I'm not going to judge you." Jack looked John directly in the eyes. "Are you going to tell me about some secret child or how I need to go through some hawk ceremony or something else that my vivid imagination's starting to think up, or are you breaking up with me?"

"Little Spirit . . . Jackson."

"Shit. You used Jackson. This is going to be very serious."

John patiently said, "No, I don't have a hidden child, there's no secret ceremony, nor would I ever break up with you."

John put his finger on Little Spirit's lips. "You promised not to interrupt, remember? Nod your head so I know you're listening to me." After Jack nodded, John continued, "Do you remember when you were on the snowmobile, and I asked you if you could hear a hawk calling?"

Jack nodded.

"Well, many hundreds of thousands of years ago, the Great Creator made all the animals, and He loved them. As time passed, He wished there were creatures more like Himself, but the souls were all used up when He made the animals. He couldn't do that. However, the animals loved Him so much, and they didn't want Him to feel alone. So some of them decided to give up their souls so He could make those more like Him. The Great Creator was so touched that these wonderful animals would make this greatest of all sacrifices just for Him that He decided that the new ones and the animals would share their souls and become one. So He made the Lakota. We're all, two together, sharing one soul. My soul's a hawk. Little Spirit, it's a very mystical and spiritual thing, and only the Lakota know of this and how it works. I'll stop for a second. Do you understand this? Now would be the time to ask questions."

Little Spirit pondered for a moment, then asked, "Are you saying you can turn into a hawk?"

John quickly replied, "No, I'm a hawk and a man together. Our spirits are one and the same. But no, I can't change into a hawk."

"Can you fly?" Little Spirit asked. "Never mind, stupid question."

John quickly responded, "There's no such thing as a stupid question at this point, I promise. So, to answer that, I can't, but my spirit hawk can. I know, see, and feel what he does, and it's the same in reverse. Together, we have the spiritual ability to move quickly and be light as a feather. It takes years of training to understand and use this ability."

Little Spirit looked as though a light had turned on in his mind. "Aww, no tracks in the snow, suddenly you're there, no one sees you when you come and go."

John looked at Little Spirit with dismay. "You've seen all of this and never asked me? Why?"

Little Spirit gave a deadpan look at his lover. "John Two Hawks, you once told me, sometimes it's better to wait and be told than it is to ask. I remembered that, and it's served me well living here with the Lakota. So, everyone has a hawk within them?"

"No, Little Spirit, each has his or her own animal spirit, and few are the same."

"So, does your dad share the soul of an elk? And does your mom share the soul of a flower? No, that wouldn't make sense."

John smiled, feeling full of love, and said, "Our names are just that, names. The tradition of naming is the same as it's been for centuries."

"So, what soul does your mom share?"

"That's something I can't share, as it's hers alone to share or not share. It's the same as for all the others."

Little Spirit's eyes sparkled with mischief, and he teased, "I'll bet money Hank's a big, fat penguin."

John burst into laughter.

"You seem to be taking this quite well. Jack, are you really okay?"

"John Two Hawks, I think this is all very incredible, I'm struggling some with it, but I also know you'd never lie to me, so I know it's true. It does explain some things. Like why that damned hawk seems to follow me around and why it's always squawking outside our house. When I'm outside wondering around, I never see it, but I sure hear it. I have to say, I'm delighted your shared spirit isn't a snake, because you definitely would have to go. But all that matters is that I love you, and nothing will ever change that, so come over here, birdman, and show me what a stud you are."

CHAPTER TEN

Suddenly, John sat up—someone was banging on the door. Then it flew open, and in stormed Jena. "Whooops!" She turned away, "1gotta learn to wait until people at least say come in." They heard the laughter in her voice.

"Ma, shut up and stay there and stay turned around!" John scolded as he and Jack scurried off to their bedroom and quickly cleaned up and got dressed. They returned to his mother.

"Why on earth don't you have your phone on?" She sounded pissed.

"Ma, what'd you want?" John said, perturbed. They're so much alike in so many ways.

"Petra Carlson's having a baby, and I need you and Little Spirit to take me there and help me deliver the baby." Jena's words demanded their assistance.

"Ma, have you lost your ever-loving mind? I don't know anything about that stuff, neither does Little Spirit! Besides—"

Little Spirit cut him off. "Oh, yes, I do. I've been at nearly every one of my nephew's or niece's births and even took classes! Let's go!" Jack geared up and got ready to go, and he practically danced out the door.

Everyone loaded into John's truck, and he took off, speeding down the road toward the destination.

Little Spirit grabbed John's arm. "John, killing us might keep you from having to help with delivering a baby, but really, is it worth it?" Little Spirit glared at him.

John quickly glanced at him and his mother. Their facial expressions were fierce enough that he slowed down.

"You told him." Jena leaned forward and talked directly to John.

"Yes, it was time." John kept his eyes straight ahead.

"Past time, if you ask me." Jena huffed. "Little Spirit, you have a hawk spirit, too. That's why he fell crazy in love with you from the moment he laid eyes on you." She squeezed Jack's hand.

"Ma, hush." John was very annoyed.

"Like he didn't know that already!" Jena teased. "So, you seem to be taking this well."

"I already knew. It's a Lakota spiritual thing. What can I say?"

They arrived in one piece. Jena raced into the small, snow-covered house. John and Little Spirit followed, carrying her equipment.

One look and Little Spirit grew white. "Good God, she's so incredibly tiny," he whispered to John.

The look on Jena's face gave nothing away. "John, call nine-one-one and see if they can get here and how long it'll take. She's closer than I thought she'd be."

"What happened here? Where's her family, her partner, or someone?"

Petra looked and him and smiled and reached her hand out. He took her hand and wiped her brow with a cold cloth.

"My parents died in a car accident when I was twenty-one," she said and panted for air. She looked barely fifteen. "My husband was buried in the cemetery last month. He was killed in Iraq and was the last survivor of his family. Little Spirit, this baby's my family. If I die, you and John must take my child. I'm giving you my son. Jena, you hear me?"

Jena nodded.

Little Spirit gently squeezed the hand and lovingly told

her, "Don't be silly. You're going to be fine. Do you have a name for him?"

"John-Lee, named for John and you, Little Spirit. The rest John will do."

Petra screamed. It sounded like it came from her very soul, and at that moment, her son came into the world. Jena acted quickly and completed the necessary things for the baby and mother.

"Ma, they're here," John said and opened the door, and the rescue squad charged into the room. John saw the looks between them. They talked with Petra and took her vitals.

"Listen to me," Petra called out. "This is the child of John Two Hawks and Little Spirit Jackson Lee McIntire!"

She went silent. The birth of her child took all her strength. The activity in the room sped up into a frenzy. Jena, the rescue squad, Petra, and her newborn son disappeared in an instant. Jack started to tear up. Obviously, his emotions had been welling up and now started to work their way out. John looked at Little Spirit, and he reached to comfort him.

The week before Christmas, they had a lull in the weather. Jack definitely wanted a Christmas tree and lights and ornaments and tinsel and more lights, so he and John went to town and shopped. John, never so much raised an eyebrow about anything Jack put in the cart.

At one point, John asked, "Little Spirit, could we have colored lights for our tree?"

Jack paused for a second. "What the heck, if you want colored lights, then colored lights it'll be."

Next, they shopped for a tree. Jack searched for nearly an hour to find the tree that they wanted.

John whined, "Little Spirit, honey, I'm freezing my nuts off, choose!"

Jack just laughed at him.

John picked up snow and threw a snowball at Jack. It hit him dead-on in the face. John looked horrified. He ran up to Jack, his voice shaky, "I'm so sorry, Little Spirit, are you hurt?"

Jack stood still in a state of shock, with eyes wide and mouth gaping. After a moment, he gathered himself and calmly wiped the snow off his face. "You didn't just face me with a snowball?" Then as quick as a wink, he took the snow he collected off his face, pulled out John's britches, and plunged the snow down the front of his pants so quickly that John never had time to stop him. "Now you're freezing your nuts off!" Jack quipped and instantly took off like a wild rabbit. He heard John's bloodcurdling, high-pitched scream, and a few seconds later, John pounced on him, and they rolled in the snow, laughed, and carried on.

"Get a room," some chuckling old man said to them.

Jack, unable to control himself, laughed out loud, but John blushed, got up, and pretended to start up the search for their tree.

There it was! Right where John had tackled him. Jack's perfectly shaped tree.

"Let's get this tree." He sounded just ever so sweet.

John replied, "Go for it." They paid for their tree and headed home.

Jack chattered away like an angry squirrel for about half the way home, but then he suddenly got silent. He turned to John. "John, I'm so sorry, I know you celebrate Christmas, but I never asked what you wanted to do or how you wanted to celebrate it. Does any of this offend you? Cuz we can take it right back, John, really. I'm truly sorry for not thinking of anyone but myself."

"Now, what are you talking about? Have I said something to make you think I was the least offended? I was with you the entire time and could've had a say in the things that you, I mean, we chose to have. Your family's coming, and you want this to be a Christmas for them and for us to remember. We'll have some of your Christmas and some of mine. It'll be wonderful. Besides, I'm not taking you back into that store for any reason. You'll be too tempted to buy more stuff. When does your family arrive? And have you told them we're living together?"

Jack paled and put on a little sickly smile.

"Are you kidding me? I can tell by the stupid look on your face that you haven't told them. Little Spirit Jackson Lee McIntire, you promised to tell them. I should make you get out and walk home."

As soon as they got to their house, Jack pulled out his phone, but before he dialed a single number, John snatched it away. "Oh no, you don't, not this time. You always sneak off and leave me to unload the truck. You're helping unload all this stuff before you get on that phone and gossip with my sister or my mother or Jason or your mother. You got it!" They brought all the stuff into the house, and Jack put his hand out, demanding his phone.

He quickly dialed. "Hi, Mom. John's got something he wants to tell you."

"No, I don't!" John said and tried to get away from the phone, but it was too late. Jack's mother was saying his name, "Hello, Melissa . . . well, no I don't really, but I'm positive Jack does."

Jack shouted out, "Mom, John and I are living together."

John looked bewildered as he listened to Jack's mother, "You know—Ohhhhh, yeah, Ma would do that—Nope, I'm not mad at her. I do love him. Sure, you can come on that day, it's fine. Watch the weather carefully, as it could change on a dime around here—Okay. Thanks, Mrs.—I mean, Melissa— yes, I'll remember, bye." He hung up and handed Jack back his phone, then immediately started to put the tree into its stand.

"What did Mom say to you? Did she really know already? What did she say to you exactly?"

"You'll have to call her yourself to get the answers to those questions."

Jack huffed at John. "It makes me so mad when you do that." Jack glared at him, but that never worked on John.

"It's driving you crazy, isn't it?" John teased.

Jack pretended all was fine, even as John watched him while he fidgeted and pace. Jack had learned right from the beginning that John would never tell him a word of any conversation he had with his mother.

Finally Jack caved, snatched up his phone, and dialed his mother again. With the call finished, Jack darted upstairs, grabbed a pillow and blanket, and handed them to John. "Looks like you'll have the couch."

John grabbed the stuff and threw it all on the couch, and picked Jack up, carried him up the stairs fireman style. "Not even my entire tribe could keep me away from you. Why would you think I'd let your mother?" They made love for half the night and again in the early morning. Thank god it snowed hard, and that meant people stayed home.

Jack and the school board had wisely called off school days before because, once again, another blizzard started. So he just spent the entire day curled up with the man he loved. "What a perfect day! John, are you okay?" Jack asked, sheepishly.

"Oh, what a perfect day. I'm so glad I spent it with you." He sang to Jack, who melted in John's arms.

That evening, John strung the lights the way Jack told him, "Back at the store, I decided to get just plain clear lights. But then your face went from happy to disappointed, so I knew a change was needed. Then you asked for colored lights, and now I'm so glad you did. I really love the multi-colored ones, and I'm so glad we bought a bunch. You're so right. They truly make our tree beautiful."

John strung the lights, and he told Jack about how the most of Lakota celebrated Christmas. John's mother practiced in the tradition of the Lakota and believed that a Lakota woman bore the son of God. The Christ child left and came back as an adult to his people and stayed for many moons. Christ talked to the people about how he suffered for all the peoples and told them how much the Great One loved the Lakota, and that the people all over the world could now enter heaven. God chose the Lakota as his special people, and the Great Creator watched over them from the beginning of time until forever.

John also told Jack how his father wasn't born on the reservation, then proceeded to tell the story that had brought him here. Thomas Three Elks' parents had been forcefully taken from their parents on the reservation and sent to a Christian boarding school. Thomas' parents hated anything considered Native American, especially Thomas' mother. She and his father never even told him about his Lakota ancestry. However, Thomas looked like a Native American, but apparently, his parents not so much. They'd told him that they'd adopted him. Thomas only found out by accident he wasn't adopted but their biological child.

He had wrecked his bike and got a brain injury. He lay in the hospital, unconscious for two days. Thomas awoke as his parents argued about the fact that they'd lied to their only son for all these years about being adopted. Thomas found that unforgivable.

Six months later, at fourteen, Thomas John Berdmen wrote a letter to his great-grandfather. He requested permission to come home to the reservation, and it was granted. The day he arrived, the entire Lakota Nation celebrated the return of one of their lost souls and welcomed him home. Great-Grandfather gave him the name Thomas Three Elks

Thomas's children never met his parents, and now that they'd passed, they never would. Thomas always loved everything about Christmas. As he told his children, "It's because I got to celebrate it with my real family from the very day I arrived here."

"He does have some beliefs like you, Little Spirit, and some like the Lakota." When John finished his story, he'd also completed the lights.

"John, you were so right about the number of lights and the color." Jack almost wanted to not put on ornaments at all. John sat down to take a look at the job he'd just finished and smiled that warm, wonderful smile of his. Jack just crawled into his lap and cuddled up with John.

Just as things had begun to heat up between them, someone knocked on the door, and it flung open. "*Oops*! Are we interrupting something?" Ma Jena gave them a naughty smirk.

John's family members flowed into their home, and they carried boxes and other things.

"Ma, Ma, Maaaa!" John's face turned red, and his eyebrows knitted.

"What, my son?"

John replied sarcastically, "What, my son? What're you, some Lakota princess from eighteen-fifty? Ma, what do you think you're doing?"

"Don't be silly. It's a tradition. We brought some of our finest things to help decorate your first tree." She looked totally perplexed.

"Ma, Little Spirit chose all these ornaments for our first tree, don't you think we —"

Jack cut him off. "Absolutely not! We can take those things

back except for the ones Mom sent us. I don't give a hoot about the others, and we need to accept these most wonderful and precious gifts."

John's smile grew. He moved directly to Jack and pulled him into his arms. "I love you more every second I know you," John whispered into his ear, then kissed it.

"You two do have a bedroom, right?" Thomas Three Elks said deadpan.

John blushed, and Jack could feel his face turn nearly scarlet red as he stepped slightly away from John.

John's family all gathered around, holding the gifts they brought for *Little Spirit* and John. John tried to sit among the crowd, but Jack wouldn't have it, so they sat together as it should be. One by one, his family offered their gifts of beautiful, handmade Lakota ornaments.

Each one was made with care and love or chosen with that same care and love. Each person explained their unique handmade ornament, and they told the story of why or how they chose it. Jack took each gift, and he and John hung them on the tree, with, of course, advice from good old Ma Jena. They shared much love and happiness that night. It took a couple of hours to complete this beautiful ceremony. It amazed Jack and touched his heart, but he held himself together like a true Lakota warrior. He thanked and hugged every single person who joined them for this celebration of love.

When everyone finished, John excused himself and came back with the box of unique ornaments that Jack's mother sent them. Jack smiled through tears up at John.

"We don't have to put those up." Jack quietly said.

"Yes! You do!" a collective voice called from John's family, echoing through the room. Jack smiled through his tears and started to hang them.

"Oh, no, you don't," Ma Jena scolded him. "Tell us why your mother sent each one."

He did just that. Each ornament symbolized every year he'd been on this planet. Some silly, some very sentimental, but all were beautiful and fit their tree perfectly.

John chose his favorite of Jack's ornaments, a silver bell with the name John engraved on it. Jack explained that his mother told his grandparents early on that they chose John for his name and Jason for his twin, but his mother changed her mind and forgot to tell everyone that they decided on Jackson instead. So when they gave it to Jack's parents, they both still believed his name was John.

"See, the Great One knew even then that you'd be in my life," John said.

"Awwwww," sounded from everyone.

"This is going to be a very special Christmas," John said and hugged Jack.

The entire McIntire clan planned to arrive three days before Christmas. John initially made plans for them to stay at a hotel about ten miles away, but Little Spirit's dad called, and they chatted about that.

Andy told John, "It isn't a money issue, but we wanted to be closer and not so far away from Jackson and you."

John talked with his mom and dad. It shocked them that he'd even thought about a hotel. His mother had already arranged where everyone stayed and who cooked where and what. Ma Jena and Melissa took care of all of that.

John asked his dad, "Did you know about all of this?"

"Of course, you dope. Do you think your mother would not involve me? Besides, how else would she be able to bark out orders for weeks at me?" They snickered until Ma Jena and Little Spirit walked into the room.

"What on earth has you two so tickled?" Little Spirit asked.

"Nothing," They both said as solemnly as they could. Ma

Jena gave them both that *Yeah-right* look, but they held it to-gether.

Chapter Eleven

John watched as the vehicles that carried Jack's family arrived in a caravan. John realized it looked almost like an invasion. Folks just stood and stared at the large crowd of new arrivals. With the looks he saw, John understood that most of the people in his tribe had never seen so many non-Native American people congregate in front of their homes. The men, women, and children piled out of the vehicles, and many of them looked an awful lot like Little Spirit.

John put his fingers in his mouth and wolf-whistled, and everyone stopped to look at him. John rounded everyone up and got their undivided attention.

John noticed that one of Little Spirit's nephews looked so sad. Tears welled up in the little guy's eyes. "What's wrong, little man?" John asked as he stooped down to speak with him.

He flung himself into John's arms and sobbed. "I thought you were really Naked Americans. But you're just betend ones."

John started to laugh but choked it back as the boy's expression looked so danged serious. "We're real Native Americans. You just watch." He picked him up and put him on his shoulders, then waved his hand high in the air and whistled. The new arrivals heard the thunder of hooves before they saw the people on horseback as they came closer and closer. They were dressed in full warrior attire — the group gasped, and the little ones clapped and cheered with excitement. The warriors, both men and women, got down from the horses and socialized with the family. Little Spirit suddenly placed his arms around John and hugged him so hard that John could barely breathe.

"Okay, everyone, let's head to the Council Hall so I can introduce my new family to my birth family," John said and herded everyone into the hall. His dad waited in the hall with the entire Council of Chiefs, all wearing full ceremonial dress. John beamed with pride. He smiled and hugged his father. "Thanks, Dad."

Introductions between the families were made. People immediately started mingling.

"John, I'm impressed! Wow! The entire family—you introduced my entire family without one single error."

"How about you introducing my entire family and extended family?"

"I live with these people. You only met my family one time just last month. That makes it impressive."

"Why Little Spirit, are you impressed? You helped by thinking each one's name as I got to that person."

Suddenly, a little pair of hands pushed them apart, and there stood little Joe-Joe, hooking his finger to have John bend down to him. He wrapped himself around John's neck and hugged him hard.

"You really are a Naked American." All around them, laughter exploded. Sounds of laughter and conversation filled the room and an indication that everyone enjoyed their time together as they got to know one another. John heard Andy McIntire's deep booming laughter as he talked with a group of people that included his parents. Little Spirit and John scanned their perfect world.

Out of nowhere, John heard Little Spirit shout, "Stop!" John looked, and he saw what Little Spirit was doing. One of the Lakota men had shoved little Joe-Joe, and the child lay on the floor with blood on his nose, screaming terror.

"John!" He felt Little Spirit's words explode in his ears. John knew Little Spirit wouldn't take this well.

John heard Iris over the crowd. "You just shoved a four-year-old child, my four-year-old child!"

She pounced on him like a wild cougar. It took Jack, Andy, and John to pull her off of him. A dozen people stepped in to help her child. When she gained her senses back, she ran to little Joe-Joe. He sobbed. His wild-eyed expression made it clear that he couldn't believe that someone had shoved him so hard.

John looked back and watched the little boy's attacker get up to his feet. There stood his best friend, Screaming Eagle. The entire council surrounded him, and John joined them. Little Spirit saw the terrible anger on John's face. He looked ready to kill his good friend.

"That little brat called me an injun. He deserves what he gets. Maybe now he'll learn we aren't a bunch of barbaric, ignorant savages."

Iris rose and handed her son to Little Spirit and moved quickly to where Screaming Eagle stood. The crowd separated. "You've proven to everyone in this place that you *are* what you said, a totally barbaric, ignorant savage. You just shoved a four-year-old baby. You're some big, brave, warrior? Let me show you just how brave you are!" Her family grabbed her and held her back.

"He did what!" Ma Jena wasn't happy.

Thomas spoke directly to Screaming Eagle. "What were you thinking? You've disgraced yourself, your family, and your entire people. You've shown no honor hurting any child, non-Native American or Native American in pure stupid anger is against everything we hold to our hearts. You're banished from our nation and our lands."

Screaming Eagle stood stunned. "For how long?" Screaming Eagle asked.

Thomas started to reply, "For a li . . ."

"No!" Little Spirit abruptly interrupted and repeated it as he shook his head, "No." He brought Little Joe-Joe to Screaming Eagle. "For whatever reason, you only saw a white child when you looked at him, and you became angry. However, he's done nothing to you. You hold onto the past like it's now, and it's not. He isn't a white child nor a Native American child, but only a child. You've broken his little spirit, and it's up to you to get him to trust and love you, or you'll have to do the other punishment."

Little Spirit handed the now squalling child to Screaming Eagle and walked away. Screaming Eagle would either have to succeed, or he'd face banishment. The anguished expression on his face showed that he didn't know what to do next.

Joe-Joe wanted nothing to do with Screaming Eagle. "Mama!" he screamed, and she reached him as fast as a lightning strike and took him, then turned and walked away, carrying her frightened child.

Joe-Joe pointed at Screaming Eagle. "You are a bery, bery bad man, and I'm going to tell your mama on you." He then buried his face into his mother's shoulder.

Keena Golden Willow shoved Screaming Eagle hard in the direction of Iris and her child. "You, big man, had better fix this and now."

He looked for help from his family and friends, but none came. "Lady, wild cat woman, wait for me," he shouted and ran to catch up with Iris.

"Man, if I were you, I'd approach her gently," John told him.

"John, don't give him advice. He needs to figure this out for himself," Little Spirit scolded.

The family get-together continued. About an hour or so later, Iris joined Ma Jena, Little Spirit, Chief Thomas, Andy and Melissa, and John.

"Where's Joe-Joe?" Melissa asked. Iris stepped aside, and there was tiny little Joe-Joe marching across the floor, his small arms folded and with that giant of a Lakota warrior half stooped following him. The group burst out into laughter.

All the while, Screaming Eagle begged for a second chance.

"How much longer?" Little Spirit asked Iris.

"Joe-Joe knows when the big hand's on the twelve, he's got to be a big boy and accept his apology, but I thought a little groveling was in order first." She winked at Chief Thomas, who threw his head back, laughing out loud.

About twenty minutes later, there were about a dozen kids that wrestled and tackled Screaming Eagle. Every one of them giggled and shrieked with delight as he went down, Joe-Joe included. The laughing smile on Screaming Eagle's face showed that he, too, was enjoying it all.

Thomas leaned in and quietly said to Little Spirit, "Good decision, my son, a very good one, indeed. I guess soon you'll be chief." He winked at John's soul mate and headed out the door.

Everyone started to head out. Joe-Joe, with a big bunch of kids along with Screaming Eagle, came up to Iris and her husband and a group of others. The group discussed the sleeping arrangements and who went where.

"Mama, Mama, Mama!" Joe-Joe interrupted.

"What," Iris spoke and was a little short with him. "Sorry baby, but you interrupted Mama when she was talking. Now, what do you want?"

"Can I sweep over with Ricky, Garrett, Mark, Lucan, Screaming Eagle, and all the rest? Please, Mommy?" Joe-Joe looked just too adorable as he begged her.

"No, tomorrow's the day before Christmas Eve, and every-one'll be too busy to watch over you. Besides, if you get homesick, there would be no one to come and get you. The snow around here's shoulder deep."

"Excuse me, Mrs. Iris, I promise he's wanted. I promise to look after him with my life, and we live across the street from John and Little Spirit, so I'd get him to you in a minute or two. Please, Iris, I need to make things up to him . . . and to you." Screaming Eagle looked her in the eye with such complete sincerity and remorse that John had to look away as tears threatened to slip out.

She looked at his pleading eyes, at her son's, then at the other children's. Then she caved. "Okay . . . but if my kid gets so much as a hangnail when you return him to me, you'll not be able to find a big enough rock to hide under." She poked her finger into his chest, then took his long hair, pulled him down to her, and kissed his cheek. "Take care of my baby boy." She whispered and started to gather the rest of her brood.

Little Spirit watched with pride, then said to John, "She has no idea that most of those boys are his, does she?"

"I'd say that's a definite, nope." John laughed in response.

Jack's family took nearly two hours to sort out who went where. The entire time, Screaming Eagle hung out on the periphery. He looked anxiously at Jack and waited for a chance to speak with him.

Finally, as things settled down, Joe-Joe brought Screaming Eagle by the hand. "Unco Jack, this man's my friend. He's very sorry and is trying to talk with you, okay?"

"Okay," Jack replied, and Joe-Joe went in search of his mother.

Screaming Eagle bowed his head low. "Little Spirit, you've loved my children like they're like your own. Having a bad day and taking it out on your little nephew was unforgivable, but you didn't let them banish me. Why not? I haven't been particularly kind to you, nor have I gone out of my way to make your friendship, but still, you stood up for me. Why?"

"Thor Screaming Eagle, your full name, correct?"

Screaming Eagle stared at him in disbelief.

"I've watched you with your large brood. You're a loving, gentle, and patient man. I've also seen you stand up in town to defend others in our community against racist bullying. What made you, such a gentle soul, go off tonight?"

"Not that this excuses my behavior, but my oldest boy, Running Fox, Drake, was beat up at the town basketball game for no reason. He's a good kid and has never been in any trouble, then he tells me the cops roughed him up a little, too." A very muffled sob came from Screaming Eagle. "Me, I get it, I was a major pain in the ass as a teenager, but my kid, no, that's just not right."

Jack took Screaming Eagle's hand and squeezed it.

"John, I need you here now," Jack calmly said.

Screaming Eagle looked at him like he'd lost his mind, but suddenly John appeared.

"How in the hell did you do that? He was nowhere to be seen!" Screaming Eagle said, somewhat surprised.

"Soulmates," John and Jack answered.

Screaming Eagle nodded that he understood. John listened to the story about Screaming Eagle's son, and he nodded that he understood, then dialed his phone as he stepped out the door.

Jack told Screaming Eagle, "You've friends and family that will always be here for you . . . use them." Then the big oaf hugged Jack.

John returned and pushed him back. "Not appropriate!"

"It was a thank you hug, you dope." Jack said as he thumped John's chest hard.

As he was leaving, John said to Screaming Eagle, "No

touching, Little Spirit, well, no hugging,"

John found Jack a short time later and explained that he'd spoken to the sheriff and the chief of police. It seemed there were issues with several of their law enforcement personnel and that some training would be in order. However, Drake Running Fox, it turned out, had made himself seem so innocent, but the truth came out. It seemed he'd been hanging around with a real raunchy crowd, into vandalism, smoking pot, and just overall bad behavior. John already informed Screaming Eagle of that news.

It pissed off Screaming Eagle when he heard the actual course of events. When Jack heard Screaming Eagle bellow his kid's name, there was definitely anger in Screaming Eagle's voice.

"That boy's going to have his father's bow across his backside tonight," John stated.

Screaming Eagle came by. "You see my boy?" The anger was still hard in his voice.

Jack took his arm. "Thor Screaming Eagle, you're majorly pissed off right now, and you're feeling bad about Joe-Joe. I get that, but you're the one that shoved that child, not Drake Running Fox. Do you get my drift here?"

"Yeah, I'm too angry to whup the daylights out of that boy tonight. However, he's going to get it, Little Spirit. He's broken the law in I'm not sure how many ways. Also, just now, his mother informed me that he's been a total shit to her and his younger brothers. Drake Running Fox lied and deceived his mother and me. He totally disrespected his wonderful mother. Plus, he did drugs! He needs to know that serious consequences follow this behavior."

John stepped into the conversation. "We make mistakes, take our punishment, and then are forgiven, right, Screaming Eagle?"

"Right," he said as his eye caught his oldest son making his way to him.

Drake walked up to his dad with a definite attitude. "Dad, whadda you want?"

Fire flamed up in Screaming Eagle's eyes. "This is how you talk to your dad? I've gotten a lot more information about what really happened tonight and about your goings-on for the last couple of months. Plus, your mother tells me you're disrespectful to her and your little brothers. Just what do you've got to say for yourself, Drake Running Fox, Mr. Attitude?"

The kid's eyes got huge, and he swallowed hard. "I'm in huge trouble, huh?"

Screaming Eagle clenched his teeth in anger. "You think? To start, you're grounded for six months for lying, six months for the pot, and six months for the pain you caused your mother. Open your mouth, and you may lose some teeth. Plus, I'll meet you in the garage tomorrow morning at six AM. sharp." Screaming Eagle poked the boy in the chest. "Do I make myself clear on this?" Drake Running Fox nodded and started to leave. "Son, you're to be in my eyeshot at all times. Any questions?"

The boy froze, then shook his head no.

Jack whispered to John, "I'm glad not to be Drake right now."

The next morning, John got up first, because he worried that his soon-to-be newly expanded family might need something. Little Spirit looked so beautiful, sound asleep in their bed that he thought it best not to wake him even though he'd promised to get him up early. John forged ahead, got coffee brewed, and started to put out all the food they needed for the people staying at their home. Ma Jena and Donna came over about five, and they started making breakfast. A group of ten planned to eat breakfast in their home.

The breakfast turned back into a gathering of families instead of a family circus. They got more acquainted and grew closer as a family unit.

Everyone congregated at the Council Hall to organize their day. A large group of women planned to Christmas shop, which left the men to mind the children and hold down the reservation.

The men and the children all went outside and played in the snow, rode snowmobiles, made snowmen, built snow forts, and had a snowball fight.

Earlier, Ma Jena informed Little Spirit, "You're mine, so let's go." No discussion, no argument, no inquiry was allowed. Little Spirit just shrugged his shoulders and followed her out.

"Ma and her secret missions!" John griped to his dad.

"But as weird as Jena's missions can be, her absence gives me some solitude . . . and don't you ever tell your mother I said that." Thomas Two Elks pointed his finger at his son.

John laughed and went out again to play with the kids. In his childhood, John always wondered where she went and what her missions accomplished, but he'd stopped trying to figure it out years ago.

CHAPTER TWELVE

What a wonderful day John and the families experienced. The kids played outside until they got cold. Then inside, they went through gallons of hot chocolate with marshmallows and hot soup with sandwiches. The hall had filled with food, children, laughter, and fathers playing with their kids, while others just stood around and talked. Everyone enjoyed the wintertime fun. The women returned in clusters and chattered away as they entered the Great Hall.

John threw Karly Little Bird DuBois, one of his sister Kitten's kids, up in the air, and when in midflight, the room suddenly went silent. John nearly forgot to catch her but did.

Then he heard Little Spirit. "John? Where are you? John?" The emotion in Jack's voice caused him to freeze.

"Jack, here I am." John worked his way through the crowd to get to Little Spirit.

"John." Jackson put his head on John's chest and sobbed the sounds of mourning. It suddenly hit John. "Where's Ma?" He was about to panic when he then spotted her. She drew close, and when she got closer, she placed her hands on Little Spirit's and John's shoulders.

Little Spirit sobbed as he said, "Petra died about an hour ago. Her little heart couldn't take the stress of childbirth. John, she made me promise to take her baby. She gave him to us. Oh, John!"

He cried so hard it hurt John's soul. Then John heard a strange sound. It sounded like a kitten at first, then grew louder.

Little Spirit stepped back and unzipped his coat, and inside, nestled all toasty and warm, was a baby. A pretty mad baby, from what John observed.

"John, I just couldn't say no to her."

"I know, love, I know. Here, give that child of yours . . . I mean ours . . . to me."

Little Spirit's hands shook, and he very reluctantly surrendered the baby.

"Don't move from this spot." John gave everyone a look that he meant them, too.

Time stood still as he took their new son to the outside world. In a second, everyone heard a loud *Boom!* Snow thunder, unusual but not rare, clapped loud and long. It startled John, the baby, and the people inside the hall. John reentered the building, raised their now screaming baby up to the Holy Father, and said, "His name is John-Lee Snow Thunder!" Everyone cheered and clapped. John walked straight up to Little Spirit, "Here's John-Lee Snow Thunder, son of Chief John Two Hawks and Little Spirit Jackson Lee McIntire, grandson of Chief Thomas Three Elks and Jena Little Flower, and grandson of Andrew McIntire and Melissa McIntire, the founders of this large and wonderful family."

John handed their precious child back to his partner in life. John saw the love in Little Spirit's expression that he already had for this child and for him. Both overwhelmed and warmed his heart.

The party exploded into the celebration of a new baby. No member of John's family tried to hold the baby or even touch it. Ma Jena explained that the child needed to bond with his parents first, then after that, they'd need a stick to keep her away. Everyone laughed, but everyone abided by what she said.

Little Spirit motioned for John to come to him. "We need baby things, like right now, things like bottles, diapers, and formula, and diapers."

"You already said diapers." John lowered his eyebrow at Little Spirit, but when Little Spirit fanned the scent of the baby toward him, reality hit John. "Yeah, he needs diapers, and like now!" The baby started to wail. Little Spirit turned to John and handed him a cranky, hungry, and very smelly baby. "Here, John, you change him while I get his supper ready."

John went into total panic mode. "What? Change him? You're kidding. Wait! Little Spirit, I don't know about this stuff. Don't leave me!" Then John turned to the men surrounding him, "Help?" Andy and the other guys gathered around, and the women just stepped back and watched. "Now, how hard can this be?" John asked Andy.

Andy gave him a look. "Man, you've no idea!"

John unfastened and peeled off the diaper. "Oh my God!" John gagged. The men all gagged and immediately took about three steps back, and the women snickered knowingly in the background.

Melissa stepped up. "Okay, I'll show you this once and once only."

"I don't think I can do this," John whined.

"Get over yourself and pay attention! This baby needs you."

"*My baby* needs me," John corrected. He followed her instructions to the letter. Through wretches and gags and a few *oh my Gods,* finally, little baby John-Lee got cleaned up and smelled like a baby, but more importantly, John claimed him as his baby boy now.

"We need a crib and clothes and . . . all the other stuff babies need," Melissa stated aloud.

Little Spirit returned with a warmed bottle. Suddenly he had a look of total surprise.

John quickly glanced back to see what had brought this on. There stood the women and men from both their families with stuff for the baby. Everything one could imagine—from homemade baby carriers to diapers, everything their son would need.

"How on earth did they gather all that stuff so quickly?" John asked Ma Jena.

"I gave Donna a heads-up before we left the hospital, and she quietly spread the word. The telling of this baby was Little Spirit's news, so everyone kept silent." Ma Jena stepped back and announced. "You're my family and the family of my newest grandson, I thank you, but take that stuff over to their home, as they'll need it there." Everything vanished as quickly as it appeared except the bag that little Joe-Joe drug over to John and Little Spirit.

Joe-Joe said, "Mama says you needed this stuff right now."

John thanked him and kissed his little head.

John's father, Chief Thomas Two Elks, raised his hand for silence, and it was immediate. "We've lost one of our precious Lakota children and also gained one. While we celebrate the birth of this child, we mourn the loss of his mother. She gave her only child to our Little Spirit and John Two Hawks, and they've claimed him as their own."

"No!" A short, elderly Native American woman pushed her way toward Chief Thomas and the baby that Little Spirit held. She was Verna Red Cloud, whose family were well known and important members of this tribe. She headed the Native American Lakota Orphan Placement Committee. "He can't claim him. He isn't Lakota, nor of our tribe." She reached for the child, which turned out to be her mistake.

"You won't touch my child!" The words spewed like venom from Little Spirit, and it scared Verna enough that she took a step back. Little Spirit's reaction startled John, too. He'd never seen Little Spirit like this. Even so, he stepped in closer.

Verna spoke up. "Ah, so you already have this babe in your

heart then. I like that, but you aren't Lakota, and the law is clear. We must first try to place every Lakota child with a willing Lakota family."

John spoke, "I'm Lakota. He's marrying me, and then he'll also be a member of the Lakota."

"But she gave her child to him. When's this marriage?" The crafty old crow smirked as though she'd one-upped him.

John whispered to Little Spirit, "No Lakota child would go to a non-member of the tribe without a huge fight." He quickly turned Little Spirit to face him. "Will you marry me right here and now? I need you to answer right now."

John held his breath for a moment. Little Spirit fired right back. "Yes, right here and now."

Little Spirit's mother shouted out, "John, you and Jackson give me a couple of hours, and I'll have my family ready for a wedding."

"Mine will be, too!" Ma Jena called out, and everyone split in all directions.

John and Little Spirit hurried home with the baby. They found all the baby things had been placed where they needed to be. John-Lee Snow Thunder was sleeping peacefully, and Little Spirit laid him in the bassinet they found set up in their room. John first kissed Little Spirit, then kissed the baby tenderly. He muttered something about the ceremony and that he needed to get some things. He took off to find those mysterious ceremonial items.

Jack laid out his best suit, tie, and shirt. He checked them for wrinkles and found the suit to be perfect to wear. He showered and shaved and was ready to get dressed.

He heard someone knocking on the bedroom door. "Come in," Jack shouted from the bathroom, but when he stepped out only wrapped in a towel to see who knocked, the room was empty. He looked around, and fear raced across his face. He shot to the bassinet that held his son, but the baby still slept peacefully. He stared at that beautiful baby boy and sighed.

He reached for his clothes, but the most beautiful white buckskin ceremonial wedding garments lay in their place. Jack could barely speak or move. The garments were decorated intricately with beads, stones, and quills. He just stared at them and ran his fingers over the delicate workmanship.

Jack's parents rapped on the door and walked into the room. They interrupted him and brought him back to reality.

"Jackson Lee McIntire, for heaven's sake, you haven't even started to get dressed!" his mother said in frustration.

He could hardly speak—finally he just pointed. "Look at what John did. Aren't they beautiful?"

Melissa urged him to get dressed. "Good Lord, son, why aren't you dressing? You're getting married in fifteen minutes. You're going to be late for your wedding. Now hurry up." She started to reach for the garments on the bed, but his dad stopped her.

"Mother, you need to leave now. I'll get our son ready." She hugged Jack, kissed her husband, and left without a word.

"How'd you do that? Mom always argues about everything and pokes her nose in absolutely everyone's business. You speak today, and poof, she's gone."

"Never mind, now get dressed. It appears your fella's been working on these garments for several weeks now. His mother told me he started on them the day you all returned from the farm. I'd say John made these with absolute love. Son, it's a wonderful wedding present. He truly loves you."

Jack started to cry. his left hand pushed up against his eyes to try and make the tears stop, but the gentle sounds of sobs came through anyway.

Jack's dad asked him, "Baby boy, why the tears on such a happy day?"

"Dad, I haven't anything to give to him in return."

"You just hush. Right now, you're giving him a son. No man could ask for more," Andy McIntire said lovingly. "Now, I'm told that John's father's helping him dress, too, and giving him sage advice. I don't know about sage advice, so the only thing I'm going to tell you is that John will be your life partner. No secrets are kept from him, and no love that comes from him is ever turned away. Put that young man first and foremost in your life always, and just love him. That's all it takes to make a good marriage."

Jack hugged his dad hard, then gathered his clothes and entered the bathroom, and he quickly dressed. He really looked so good in the ceremonial clothes that John had made him. Thanks to John, they were a perfect fit.

When he stepped out for his father to see him, Andy took one look at him, and through the happy tears of a proud father, he said, "You're my son, I love you, I'm so proud of the man you are."

John-Lee stopped all the weepy emotions with one little squawk. They both charged to the bassinet, colliding heads in the process. Laughter filled the room.

"Damn, son, your head's hard as a rock," Andy teased.

Mary and Mae arrived to do childcare. Mae took one look at Jack, and her smile burst forth. "You're just so beautiful. Now get out! If you don't hurry, you'll be late for your wedding."

The two men threw on their coats and hurried to the hall. The cold wind blew the snow around in circles in front of them. When Jack and his father arrived at the hall, it only had two torches lighting the doorway. Darkness filled the inside of the building. A Lakota warrior met them inside with a flaming torch, dressed up in all the Lakota's finest, as if he were ready for battle. When he spoke, Jack realized that Hank was leading them into the hall. Someone took their coats and indicated for them to continue to follow Hank.

Hank led them to the left side, where Jack's family waited for them. He heard a commotion on the other side but couldn't see what was going on. Suddenly, everything went totally dark. A lone woman started chanting slowly, and others joined her. Hank told Jack's family that the entire nation prayed for a perfect union of body, mind, and spirits.

Then Hank side-mouthed to Jack, "I heard the body part is already unionized."

It became silent again. In an instant, the center of the room was lit with torches.

There stood Tȟuŋkášila Waŋblí decked out in his finest, standing straight and proud. He spoke first in Lakota, then broken English. "Why have you summoned me to come here?"

The torches on both sides lit up. "We ask that you do the *Kichiyuzapi* ceremony for my son and your great-grandson, John Two Hawks, Tȟuŋkášila Waŋblí," Chief Thomas requested.

Jack's father stepped forward. "And we likewise ask the same for our son, soon to be your great-grandson, Little Spirit Jackson Lee McIntire, Tȟuŋkášila Waŋblí." Jack smiled at his father's dignified demeanor.

"Those who are of like mind, body, and spirit come to me, but come only with a full heart and without any regrets or indecision."

Jack walked quickly toward Tȟuŋkášila Waŋblí. About halfway there, he spied John, who was dressed just like him. John looked so very handsome in his wedding attire. Jack almost stopped just to look at him. John's face was washed clean without any ceremonial paints. With only a few feet between them, Tȟuŋkášila Waŋblí stopped them. "That part comes after the wedding." Then he laughed at his own joke. He froze and looked out, annoyed at the crowd. Only then did others get the hint to laugh, too. His playfulness indicated that he was enjoying performing this ceremony.

Even with Tȟuŋkášila Waŋblí's somewhat broken English, he got his point across about what marriage had to be. "You'll be needing to have love, trust, understanding, and above all, patience."

Great-grandfather pointed at the sacred paints and told Jack what to do. "Take and dip your two fingers in the black paint, make two lines over each of John's eyebrows, and one down the middle of each cheek." Jack did as he was told. "Next, dip one finger in the red paint and make one line on each side of the black lines on John's cheeks and one line in between the black lines on his forehead."

"Good job, my child. Two Hawks, you must listen carefully, for you won't do the same. Take one finger and make one black line from his hairline to the middle of his eyebrow on each side, then do two black lines down the middle of his cheeks, then do one red line on each side of the forehead's black lines and one red line in between black lines on his cheeks, these two are compliments of each other yet different, the same and apart," Tȟuŋkášila Waŋblí said. John followed his instructions.

"Two Hawks, are you of the mind to take Little Spirit as your soul mate and life partner?"

"Yes, Tȟuŋkášila Waŋblí, I am."

Tȟuŋkášila Waŋblí's eyes went very wide. "Tell your young man, not me!" He then laughed, and the people in the room chuckled with him.

John looked sheepish. "Yes, Little Spirit. I do take you as my soul mate and life partner."

"And you, little man, now known as Little Spirit, are you taking Two Hawks as your soul mate and life partner? Think carefully . . . he doesn't appear to be so bright," Tȟuŋkášila Waŋblí said with a naughty twinkle in his eye. The room filled with a rumbling of snickers.

"It makes no difference, Tȟuŋkášila Waŋblí. Two Hawks, I do take you as my soul mate and life partner."

Tȟuŋkášila Waŋblí clasped his hands on the wedding couple and announced for all to hear, "I say they're now joined as one!"

Torches lit up all around the room, and warm light filled it. The entire hall was filled with people. The chanting and drums started again, and everyone joined in. John began to dance in a circle. Little Spirit just stared at him but saw the happiness in each step that John moved.

Tȟuŋkášila Waŋblí told Little Spirit, "He's dancing for joy, and you must, too."

Little Spirit did just that. The dancing and chanting seemed to go on and on and got louder and louder. However, just as abruptly as it started, it stopped.

John let out a whoop and grabbed Little Spirit's hand. John ran him to Little Spirit's parents, and loving emotions erupted as all the McIntires hugged them both.

John again took his hand and ran him this time to his parents, again with hugs and happiness all around.

Little Spirit then thumped John's chest. "You need to stop that! I could've walked without you dragging me, but oh no, you just had to warrior up, didn't you?"

John laughed. The lights brightened more, and the wedding feast began. Little Spirit's little nephews and nieces went over the top with excitement over all the ceremonial paint and wardrobes.

Joe-Joe told Little Spirit, "This proves that John and his family really are Naked, no, Naaative Americans now for sure."

John quickly arranged for all of the little kids to have their faces painted, and the little ones squealed with delight.

Little Spirit's telephone alarm rang. He took one look, and he started to dart out of the room. John looked perplexed and tried to stop him. Little Spirit signaled he'd be right back.

Within a few minutes, Little Spirit walked in with their son. Mary and Mae had dressed him in beautiful Lakota baby clothes that matched the grooms.

John took baby John-Lee Snow Thunder. "Meet my new son, John-Lee Snow Thunder. He'll someday be a great chief."

Tȟuŋkášila Waŋblí stood, and everyone went silent. "No, he won't be a great chief. He'll be a great holy man and healer of our people."

Chief Thomas placed his hands on Little Spirit's shoulders and whispered, "There's no higher honor than that in the Lakota Nation."

Little Spirit turned to look at Chief Thomas and saw the great pride on his face. Unexpectedly, John scooped Little Spirit up to stand next to him. Little Spirit took their baby back before the poor little thing got accidentally tossed out to the crowd, and John embraced him with such love and tenderness. The *aah's* floated through the room.

The shock of what was happening hit Little Spirit, and he did the fish mouth thing until John elbowed him. "Little Spirit, you got that fish mouth thing going again. What's wrong?"

Little Spirit looked at John and said, "I just came to the realization that I'm a married man with a newborn baby." Little Spirit raised his left hand high up to the heavens. "Thank you for your blessings, Great One. Thanks for your love, and thank you for all you've given us."

A collective *Amen* echoed around the room. The celebration ended in the wee hours of the morning.

Chapter Thirteen

Jack hadn't planned for a wedding as part of their Christmas celebration. He wanted to make a proper blending of both families' holidays. It never happened the way he planned. None of his organized plans turned out to be important because, somehow, things just all happened anyway. It suddenly turned into only about family. Nothing else mattered.

Christmas Eve evening had arrived, and the families split. Little Spirit's mom made it quite clear that they all needed to attend Mass, so the entire McIntire clan got ready to set off for St. Anne's Catholic Church. The skies had cleared, and no snow was forecast until late in the evening the day after Christmas Day. Little Spirit expected John to stay with his family, but John came out dressed in a suit and carrying their son to the car. He put the baby and the car seat in the back seat of the car like a pro and got in. Little Spirit was a bit shocked.

Little Spirit's surprised look made John laugh. "What did you think? You'd go to church without me?" Little Spirit shook his head no. John finally figured out Little Spirit's puzzlement. "Oh, the car seat. I'm becoming a baby expert," John told him as he kissed Little Spirit's nose.

The church looked to be huge for this small community, but it turned out to be just about right. Little Spirit's mom and dad led the entire clan up front and took the empty seats. When they finally settled, Little Spirit heard some commotion behind him. But baby John-Lee was fussing, and all of Little

Spirit and John's attention went to that precious baby.

The priest walked into the sanctuary and introduced himself. "Hello, everyone. I'm Father Henry. Merry Christmas to you all!"

All in attendance replied, "Merry Christmas!"

Father Henry sounded jovial and warm. "It's my understanding we've a new member of this very large family." Father Henry smiled.

Little Spirit's parents nodded and smiled toward little John-Lee, John, and Little Spirit. "Who brings this child to be baptized in this church?" Little Spirit was completely caught off guard by what the priest said. He and John had never discussed baptism or any aspect of the religious upbringing of their child. Even more shocking was the considerable reply that echoed all over the church, "We do!" Little Spirit turned, and there sat all of John's family. Jena and Thomas beamed at him. It looked as though half of the tribe was in attendance.

A very surprised Little Spirit looked to his husband. John smiled and shrugged. "No one dared argue with our mothers. Melissa and Ma discussed this and came to the conclusion that John-Lee would grow up knowing both cultures. So baptism was okay with Ma."

"Don't you think I should've been involved in that discussion, too?"

"You tell our mothers that."

Father Henry walked up to John and Little Spirit. "Who'll be this child's spiritual godparents?"

John looked to Little Spirit. "Who do you think?"

"I'd like to ask Donna Yellow Bird and Iris to be his godmothers and Hank and my brother Jason to be his godfathers. Screaming Eagle, could you stand in for Jason, as he isn't here and be a third godfather? Is that okay with you, John?" John smiled and agreed.

Hank at first looked startled, then overwhelmed, so much

that all he could do was nod.

The baptism ceremony and the rest of the service finished beautifully. Plus, having the families all gathered together on this special occasion made it complete. When Mass ended, the blended family all wished each other Merry Christmas, then dispersed.

As his father carried him out of church, a very sleepy Joe-Joe asked, "Did Santa come yet?"

"No, baby, not yet." His mother kissed his sleepy head, and he drifted back into slumberland to dream of the magic of Christmas.

When they arrived home, the first thing Little Spirit did was settle a sleeping John-Lee in his cradle. He then went to get cleaned up and ready for bed. When he finished in the bathroom, he stepped out into the bedroom, and John Two Hawks lay on the bed. He looked so damn hot that Little Spirit nearly stumbled.

John chuckled. "Uh, watch where you're going. I don't want you breaking something important that we need on our second night of marriage." He waggled his eyebrows, "Little Spirit, why'd you choose my sister Donna and your sister Iris for godmothers? And Screaming Eagle, Jason, and most surprisingly, Hank, for godfathers?"

"Do you disapprove?" Little Spirit looked worried.

John shook his head. "Absolutely not. I agree with your choices. But why'd you choose them?"

"Because I knew that they'd fight to the death to protect our son."

Christmas morning came, and John got up and out of the house before dawn. John asked everyone who could help him to move everything to the hall so that all the families could be together. The move proved a huge undertaking but well worth the effort. The children and their parents swarmed into the hall. Family groups gathered around their own Christmas trees, and one massive tree stood in the center for all.

The *oohs* and *ahhs* came from all directions. The children were over the moon excited.

Little Spirit gave John a pair of black jeans, a beautiful sweater, and stocking stuffers. John gave Little Spirit a new briefcase, a pair of beautiful beaded moccasins, and a 14kt gold wedding band. The day was perfect, and the families blended so nicely.

Christmas was over, and Jack's family packed up and left.

He and John would now get the needed time to bond more with their new son.

Finally, peace and quiet settled throughout the reservation.

Chapter Fourteen

A few days before school started back, Little Spirit announced, "I'm seriously considering not going back to school. I don't want our son to go to daycare."

John looked at him for a second, then burst into uncontrolled laughter. "Dr. McIntire Two Hawks, you have a contract, and I promise you, no one will let you out of it. Besides, who would you turn the school over to? Hank?"

"Hank! Oh my God, he can be such a jerk. That's a big no! Okay, Mr. *I'm in charge*. Who's going to take care of John-Lee?"

John knitted his eyebrow and at first just stared. "Me, of course."

Having just taken a sip of coffee, Little Spirit spat it all over. "You? The one that gagged at even the thought of changing a diaper? The guy that tried to give a newborn venison jerky? The guy that drove fifteen miles one way to have his mother change his son's diaper, who, by the way, was in town shopping? You think you should be the one to take charge of our baby? You're joking, right?"

"Okay, I was a bit awkward with John-Lee at first, I admit that, but now I'm a super dad! By the way, when's this kid going to be able to eat real food? Have you tasted that baby formula? I could puke." John gave Little Spirit those big brown doe eyes and that heart-melting smile.

"John, he doesn't have teeth yet. He's a newborn. They'll come soon enough, and believe me, we'll know when that happens. Until then, he'll be on formula for some, but mostly he's on donated breast milk. Which he will be for several months to come."

"Don't be so smug. I was raised to be a superior warrior, not mother superior." Little Spirit's face definitely showed that John's sarcasm didn't go over very well. "Sorry, Little Spirit, no, I'm sorry. That was an idiotic remark. It was meant to be funny. I guess not so funny, huh? Please don't be mad at me." Again, with the eyes and smile, Little Spirit caved.

"Okay, until I go to school, you'll be in charge, just to see if you can handle this. From now on, you have seven AM to five PM duty, and we'll see, Mr. Hotshot Superior Warrior, if you can handle this."

"Great, give me my son. I've got to get him bundled up and ready to go. Some of the guys' are snowmobiling to the bison herd to see how they're faring." He reached for their son.

Little Spirit firmly informed him. "Absolutely not! This tiny little guy will have to wait for such an adventure, and his dad will have to forgo it, too. Seeing as this is his time to tend to our son. Am I clear on that subject? John, do you hear me?"

John sat there with his staring at Little Spirit like he could not understand his words. "Just when will my son be able to do all the fun stuff with me?" He demanded.

"In a couple of years."

"Years! Are you kidding me? Years?" John sounded and looked stunned.

"John, you're a twenty-seven-year-old man, highly educated, and a very important chief. You've lived here and among your family your entire life. How on earth did you miss out on child-rearing?" His words made John stop and think.

"I just never had to think about it. Someone else had that responsibility. But now, I guess, that responsibility's mine." John paused for a long moment. Then sounding almost panicky, said, "Little Spirit, what if I hurt him or, even worse, forget where I put him or leave the house without him? No . . . I can do this, I want to do this, and he needs me. With your help, Ma's, and Kitten's, too, I can do this, I promise."

John stepped up and did what he promised, and he did it quite well.

Little Spirit found it hard to believe that John could do what he believed. But, without a doubt, he came through like a true trained warrior. Little John-Lee flourished under John's nurturing and loving care. He grew and learned to say words, then sentences.

Spring had come and gone, as did summer and fall. John-Lee crawled early, and he walked before he was a year. He suddenly just stood up and toddled over to John. From that moment on, he became John's shadow. Little Spirit swore that he walked very early so he could go with John.

John-Lee soon walked like John and stood like him, and he even talked like John. John-Lee potty trained very early, too. John bragged about how he should write a book about parenting. Suddenly, he looked at John-Lee, scooped him up, and ran for the potty.

"John, you know that he really isn't potty trained, right? You're potty trained! If you hadn't been extra observant, he would've had an accident."

John fired back, "Whatever works, Little Spirit, is what I'll use. So I don't have to change those godawful diapers!"

People all over the reservation were tickled as they watched them grow and become more and more alike every day.

The spring after John-Lee turned two, Little Spirit watched from the porch and tried to figure out why John-Lee was having a private tantrum in the front yard. John came up from behind and wrapped his arms around Little Spirit.

"John, did something happen today while I was at work?"

"No. Why?"

"Then why's John-Lee having a major tantrum out in our front yard?"

"Tantrum? That isn't a tantrum. He's doing his war dance. Can't you see that?"

Little Spirit sat down and started laughing. The more little John-Lee danced, the harder Little Spirit laughed. Finally, Little Spirit caught his breath and looked at John, and said with all sincerity, "He dances like someone put a cactus in his pants."

John looked up at John-Lee, back at Little Spirit, then back at John-Lee. "He does, sort of, doesn't he?"

The two of them watched through laughter.

Chapter Fifteen

The Christmas after John-Lee turned three, he started to fully participate and understand the holiday festivities. Much excitement filled in the air. Shopping, decorating, and presents under the tree all made him happy and excited.

At one point, John-Lee had a very long private chat with Santa. John-Lee brought the spirit of Christmas home to them all.

On Christmas morning, the impact of his innocent belief in the magic of Christmas came to life. Every present he opened thrilled him, but he kept looking for something else. "This is very way cool, but it's not what I asked Santa Claus for." He'd say without malice but just a little disappointed. Little Spirit looked to John for the answer, and he just shrugged and whispered, "I thought we knew everything he wanted." When John-Lee got to the very last present, it was a big, beautifully wrapped box. He first listened to it, then looked horrified.

He turned frantically to John. "Dad, help me quick, he can't breathe!" The two of them tore it open quickly, and inside, there was the buffalo stuffed animal he'd so desperately wanted just three weeks ago. They agreed that he should have it as it represented his animal spirit. He looked up at Little Spirit with huge tears, jumped up, and ran to him sobbing. "Santa forgetted all bout me. Daddy, he promised me and then forgetted." He buried his head on Little Spirit shoulder and sobbed uncontrollably.

Little Spirit first saw John's embarrassment, then John's anger starting to rise. Their child seemed unhappy with everything the families and gotten him.

Little Spirit whispered to John, "John-Lee isn't a greedy and self-centered child. He's always been gentle and shares what he has."

John took him from Little Spirit. "John-Lee, you got so much from everyone that loves you. Santa even brought you that wonderful stuffed bison. Are you not grateful for all the things they gave you?"

He sniffled and sputtered, "I love everything I getted bery much, but Santa promised, Dad."

"Promised what, son?"

"For me to get a baby brother." He howled and started sobbing again.

John scowled. "Little Spirit, why on earth would he do that?"

"John, I got this. John-Lee, look at me."

He raised his little tear-stained face and looked at his Dad and Daddy.

"Son, Santa doesn't deliver babies, and you know that. Who around here delivers most of the babies?"

"Gramma Jena, Aunties Mary and Mae do." His expression changed like a light came on in his little head. He got down and rushed to Jena, one hand on his hip and the other shaking a scolding finger at his grandmother. "Gramma! What have you done with my baby brother?"

"Well, my precious grandson, he just isn't born yet, not until early February." It only took a second for her to realize that she'd let a well-guarded secret out of the bag. "Oops! Sorry, John, Little Spirit. I didn't mean to blab so soon. I mean, oh heck, you know what I mean. I'm just so sorry."

All eyes turned to John and Little Spirit. Little Spirit's mother looked a bit shocked. The family moved closer to John and Little Spirit. Everyone started asking questions about what was going on.

John's protective side flared up, and he started crowd control. "Please, you all need to settle down. This information is news we planned on sharing a bit later."

John-Lee asked, "So am I getting baby bwover or not?"

John cleared his throat to speak, but the family started to split.

In the background, they heard Donna. "Get out of my way, move it buster, step aside." No one had really noticed her pregnant bulge until that moment. "Okay, you nosy busybodies, Two Hawks, Little Spirit, Sally Anne, and I are expanding our families. As you can see, I'm huge even for me. I'll, or rather, we'll be having a little girl and a little boy in February, if all goes right. John and Little Spirit get the boy, and Sal and I get the girl. I know it sounds like horse trading, but it was all done with the utmost love. So let me inform you all. You've enough business of your own, so don't be minding ours!" She turned and walked over to the big comfortable chair and fell into it.

Everyone's attention left her and turned to John and Little Spirit. "Okay, we, John and I, planned to expand our family, and Donna and Sally Anne agreed to help. When the baby was discovered to be twins, FYI, I'm the father to both, John and I decided to share our blessing. Which would enable Donna and Sally Anne to have a baby of their own too. They chose the baby girl but only if John and I agreed to have another child soon. We agreed. So now you know the entire story."

The silence seemed to be deafening. Little Spirit's mom spoke first. "So am I getting one or two grandchildren out of this deal?"

Donna smiled. "You'll be getting two. No child can have too many interfering and loving grandmothers." Everyone laughed except for their son, John-Lee. He sat there and fumed. His face said it all—this wasn't what he thought would happen.

John asked him, "Why the big pout, son?"

"Santa isn't very smart when it comes to getting babies," he angrily told John.

The spirit of Christmas returned to the room.

John-Lee remembered that he had a new collection of wonderful toys, so he went off and played with them.

Chief Thomas Three Elks walked up and hugged first John, then Little Spirit. He then gave Jena a look. "How's it that all this stuff goes on, and I know absolutely nothing about it?"

"Well, my beloved husband, I'm more than happy to fill you in on all the reproductive matters of this nation. Now where should I start?"

Thomas paled, then very calmly stated, "Never mind, old woman, never mind."

Jena's smiling face turned to a scowl in a split second. "Who are you calling an old woman?" Jena snarled, and Thomas made a hasty retreat.

Jena started searching for something. "Hey, someone moved my spoon." She scurried to the kitchen to find it.

Donna shifted slightly, raised the spoon just enough for Little Spirit to spy it, then hid it back down. They shared a secret smile. Poor Jena, everyone conspired to rid her of that damnable spoon.

Andrew Thomas Grey Owl and his cousin-sister Melissa Jena Snowbird came into the world without incident. Both were healthy, and everything seemed right with the world. Well, almost. Before the babies were born, John, Little Spirit, Donna, and Sally Ann had discussed the babies. The four of them decided to keep the babies together for a little while. They chose John and Little Spirit's home because they had the most room. Everything they'd read indicated that twins could suffer from separation anxiety if kept apart.

The babies fussed and cried all the time. The couples begged Jena to help them, but it perplexed her, too. They even called the doctor to examine them and see if he could help. He found nothing wrong, medically at least.

One week after their birth, Thomas came by to see the babies, and they squalled the entire time.

"Lord, is this going on all day and night?"

"Yes!" Both Donna and Little Spirit said, and they sounded desperate.

Then Donna got up to change Lisa. As soon as she left the room, it became instantly quiet. No one had ever really noticed that. Donna and Lisa reentered the room, and the squalling started again.

Thomas spoke, "Donna, take that child out into the kitchen." The moment she left the room, both babies were silent. "Come back now," Thomas called out to her. The second she got back, it started up again. "It's plain they do not like each other. Keep them separated."

"Now that you mention that . . ." Little Spirit looked from Thomas to Donna. "Donna, the last month you were pregnant, you were always complaining that they were at war inside you."

"That's so true."

As it turned out, not all twins suffered from separation issues.

Andrew Grey Owl was an easy baby for John and Little Spirit but a huge disappointment for his big brother.

"Dad, all he does is cry, eat, poop, and pee. He can't talk or nothing. I think he's broked."

Little Spirit and John told the broked story over and over again. Absolutely every time they repeated it, people found it hilarious, too.

John proved to be the best of stay-at-home-working dads.

He raised their sons to be disciplined warriors. He taught them that patience and kindness were virtues that all warriors needed. He mostly taught by example as they watched and learned. John-Lee followed John around the entire reservation and became more and more like his dad. John went about his daily duties but always with their children in tow. So many people teased him about being a wonderful mother. He never even flinched. John loved being a dad, loved his kids, and loved Little Spirit.

Andy flourished and adored his big brother. John-Lee learned to be the world's best big brother and spent much of his time teaching Andy everything he knew. Everyone swore Little Andy walked and talked so early just to keep up with John and John-Lee. Andy's adoration of his big brother came early. Even his first word had been WaaWee, his name for John-Lee. Andy called him that for months.

As Andy grew and gained his independence, he turned out not quite as easy-going as everyone thought. Stubbornness showed more and more as he grew. "He definitely got that from Little Spirit's side of the family," John told his friends and family.

Andy and John butted heads all the time. "Andy, you need to pick up your toys now and get ready for dinner."

"No, Dad, you do it."

"I'm not going to pick up your mess. Now get busy."

"Don't holler at me," Andrew sassed with his hands on his hips.

Little Spirit just happened to round the corner and saw this entire confrontation. Little Spirit's temper flared. "Andrew Thomas Grey Owl, you're never allowed to talk to Dad like that. Do you understand me?"

He looked at Little Spirit and talked back. "Mind your own business."

John had to turn away, so Andy wouldn't see he was

holding back the laughter

Little Spirit, on the other hand, saw absolutely nothing funny about their son's bratty behavior. He snatched him up and swatted him on his behind.

"That didn't hurt," Andy popped off. However, the next three sure enough did, and he wailed so loud the neighbors could hear him.

"That's about enough of that, little man. You sound like you need a couple more swats."

"No hitting! Dad, save me. Daddy's too mean for me," Andy pleaded.

"You're on your own here, buddy," John quipped and left.

"Pick up these toys now." Little Spirit meant business.

"My am!" Andy shouted and held only one small toy but stood, not moving.

"My not! Move it!" Little Spirit demanded back.

Andy picked up with a fury, and when he finished, Andy looked at Little Spirit. "I don't like you, not one little bit."

"Really, well, I still love you bunches," Little Spirit said back and walked back to the kitchen, where he found John.

Peals of laughter came from John. "My am, my not, I think I'm going to pee myself, Mister Doctor of Education."

"Okay, maybe I stooped down to Andy's level, and he does have pronoun issues at times. I admit that it wasn't necessarily the best parenting example, but it worked, didn't it?"

"Daddy, I need you!" Little Spirit found him in the living room. Andy stood with his arms raised for him to pick him up, and his daddy did. "I am very sorry, Daddy," he said, and laid his head on Little Spirit's shoulder.

"I know you are, Andy, but you've got to mind your dad. Do you understand that?"

"No, I don't. He never gibs smacks. Only you do, Daddy."

John called out from the kitchen, "Don't hold your breath there, boy. I know about spanking, just ask your brother."

Andy got wide-eyed at looked at his big brother, who only nodded and rubbed his backside.

Little Spirit could hear John in the kitchen laughing again. "My am, my not . . . from Mister Educator." His laughter faded as he went out of the house. John left to spread the story he thought so hilarious.

John and Little Spirit's lives became everything that they dreamed they could be. Their children grew, as did their independence.

At the end of the summer, John-Lee learned he was going to attend kindergarten. They visited the school, saw his kindergarten classroom, and met his teacher. His excitement grew as the opening day came closer. But only until John-Lee discovered kindergarten class lasted all day and not just part-time like school last year.

He instantly made up his mind. "Dad, I decided not to go to Daddy's school and just stay home."

"Nope, son, you're going to school. It's not an option and not open to discussion."

The world stood still for about one second, and just as Little Spirit walked through the front door, John-Lee exploded into the most magnificent tantrum ever seen on the entire reservation. John-Lee screamed and threw himself on the floor, kicked and cried, slammed his little fists on the floor, then screamed some more.

John turned red and felt about to explode with anger, but Little Spirit grabbed his arm and stopped him. Little Spirit shook his head and held his hand up to indicate that John needed to stay put. After at least five full minutes, John-Lee got tired and started to quiet down.

Little Spirit applauded and cheered. "What a magnificent tantrum, John-Lee."

John immediately caught on and said the same thing.

At first, John-Lee sat there and stared at them both. He looked confused. Then he said with a scowl, "That's not the right answer. You were supposed to say I could stay home and not go to that terrible school of yours."

Little Spirit smiled sweetly at him and said, "That didn't work, nor is it going to work. Are you finished now? Or do you need more baby time?"

The baby time thing hit John-Lee hard. "I am not a baby!" John-Lee glared at them both. Then his expression went from angry to serious. "I'll pack my own book bag without your help."

"Of course, you're a big boy. You know how to do that."

John-Lee scurried off.

"Little Spirit, you amaze me sometimes," John said as he sat down, grabbed Little Spirit around the waist, pulled him onto his lap, and kissed him.

"Ewwww, kissing, yuck! Daddy, do you think sixty-eighty pencils are enough?" John-Lee said.

"You only need four pencils," Little Spirit answered.

John-Lee smiled, turned around, and headed back to his book bag packing.

John looked at Little Spirit. "Four? Why four? Also, how much is sixty-eighty?"

"He can count them out and correctly get that amount, and that keeps this *his* book bagging project. Sixty-eighty would be every pencil he could find in the house."

John laughed and said, "I get that. That was the biggest tantrum I've ever seen. How on earth did you keep it together like you did?"

Little Spirit chuckled as he said, "Seriously, I was just about to join him on the floor with the kicking and screaming. God, he's just as bullheaded and stubborn as you are."

Little Spirit moved quickly to be out of John's reach. "Who

are you kidding? That was you all over. Well, maybe a little me, too." The two of them both smiled, and John pulled Little Spirit close.

Chapter Sixteen

School started very smoothly, albeit very hot for September. John busied himself with their littlest one and the business of running the reservation while Little Spirit efficiently ran the school.

Little Spirit sat at his desk and pondered how things went so smoothly. When Donna came into the office, he remarked, "Maybe school's going a little too smoothly."

Donna said in response, "The moment you think that, you're putting bad vibes into the air."

Suddenly the sirens blared—a tornado!

Donna and Little Spirit immediately jumped into action.

Little Spirit blurted out as he shot out of the office, "Kids play on the playground this time of the day." He told Donna, "Secure the school and get set for the worst." He flew past her on his way outside to the play area. Teachers and students were on a dead run, racing into the building. Little Spirit hollered for teachers to be sure and account for every child and get them to the safety of the tornado zones in the building.

Kara Dancing Flower, a new kindergarten teacher's assistant, shouted to Little Spirit, "I don't have John-Lee or Junie!"

Little Spirit shot out onto the playground. Desperate to find the two babies, he scanned the playground. He screamed at the top of his lungs, "John-Lee, Junie, where are you? Answer me, John-Lee!"

The storm started to hit, the wind picked up, and it was starting to rain. The sound of roaring wind drowned him out, so he picked up his pace and ran to the back of the playground. He frantically searched. Finally he spied a small pink shoe under the slide. He pulled them from under underneath. "Come, babies, we need to run!" The slide offered them no protection. He picked them up and ran with every ounce of strength, and he pushed through the storm toward the school. He nearly lost hold of John-Lee, but he quickly regained his grip.

"John *Núŋp Čhetáŋ*, where are you?" he screamed into the storm, and John appeared, took John-Lee, engulfed them all into his arms, and protected them from the debris that was now flying through the air.

When they hit the doors, Little Spirit and John quickly handed the children into the waiting arms of teachers, who stood just inside. The teachers disappeared with the children as fast as they got them.

Little Spirit turned back and took one last look. The tornado hit, pulling him out of the doorway. John grabbed him and held on tight to the metal center divider of the door with one hand and Little Spirit with his other.

Little Spirit screamed, "Don't let go!"

John never let go, and at the slightest let up in the storm, he yanked Little Spirit and himself back into the building. Hand in hand, they then fled to the shelter. Both were covered with tornado shrapnel, and some of the stuff had pierced their skins, but they'd survived.

"Don't you ever scare me like that again!" John gently pulled him in close. Little Spirit and John clung together. The tornado finally passed.

Jena Little Flower appeared with her medical team and treated all the minor injuries.

Donna reported to them. "Everyone's safe and accounted for, and there were zero child injuries. A few teachers did get simple scratches."

Jena ordered John and Little Spirit to go into the emergency room at the hospital as she felt some of the debris needed to be removed by the doctor. Neither protested,. They both just had minor debris removed. They extremely sore when they got back home that evening. Jena gave them an herb salve to rub on each other's sore muscles and joints and another salve for the cuts.

"You know, John, we've had blizzards, thunderstorms, hail, flooding rain, and now a tornado. The only thing we haven't had is . . . ." John clasped his hand over Little Spirit's mouth.

"Just don't put anything else into the air, please."

Not a single life was lost that day, and although plenty of damage occurred to the homes and buildings, all proved repairable. The school came through it untouched.

When people saw that tornado's path had crossed right through the school and then saw it unscathed, many sincerely thought that Little Spirit's great love for their children protected the entire building and everyone in it.

Later that week, when all had settled and most of the repairs were finished, the whole reservation met in the Great Hall. Prayers and thanksgivings were said. The people thanked the Great Spirit that no one got severely hurt and that damage to the structures turned out minimal.

Screaming Eagle stood, and everyone became silent. "Man called Little Spirit." Little Spirit looked at him startled, but Screaming Eagle continued, "We've all come to love you, and we believe that your great love of our children covered the school with protection and saved them." Screaming Eagle's voice contained much emotion. "You saved them, and John saved you. The Great One has smiled on us all and blessed us, and we thank you."

Little Spirit said nothing—he just stood closer to John. Emotions hung heavily in the air.

Chief Thomas Two Elks broke the silence. "Enough, it's time to celebrate that once again, this great nation's survived another near catastrophe. Let's dance and sing with joy."

Dance, they all did, and they danced with joy. Little Spirit danced with everyone else.

Hank danced by, and he commented, "You dance like a bird walking on hot coals." He laughed and just continued.

John heard Hank and retorted, "And you dance like a fat penguin." Hank laughed out loud.

Laughter and happiness surrounded them.

CHAPTER SEVENTEEN

Another Christmas was upon them. John, Donna, Sally Anne, and Little Spirit announced that John and Little Spirit were expecting their third son, and Sally Ann and Donna were getting a second daughter. John and Sally Anne were responsible for the son. Donna and Little Spirit were responsible for her and Sally Anne's baby daughter, all due sometime in mid-March.

Thomas Three Elks took Little Spirit aside. "I'd have never thought you and John would allow each other to take up with someone else."

Little Spirit's facial expression went from jovial to grave. "Thomas, have you lost your mind? We didn't participate. We donated. If you catch my meaning."

"Good God, way too much information flowing here. I need to learn to keep my thoughts to myself," Thomas said as he hurried away before Little Spirit could say anything else.

Babies Jacqueline Blue Jay and Jackson Red Hawk were born without incident just seven days apart. Jay-Jay came into the world just perfect. Born tiny and petite with her dark black hair and dark skin and Little Spirit's emerald green eyes. Jackie, in spite of his beautiful features, turned out neither a quiet nor a cuddly baby. Plus, he only wanted to be held by Little Spirit. He squalled his head off every time Little Spirit so much as tried to put him down.

Screaming Eagle commented to John, "Jeez, can Little

Spirit even go to the bathroom without that kid shrieking?"

John replied, "That kid's wearing us all out. But Little Spirit's on the brink of exhaustion. To tell the truth, I know just how that baby feels. I want to be held by him all the time, too."

Screaming Eagle nodded that he understood, as he'd watched his friend fall so deeply in love. "John, we've all seen that great love you have for each other."

"I'm pretty sure that Little Spirit keeps this heart of mine beating."

"I have a feeling that Little Spirit feels the same way." Screaming Eagle jokingly punched John's shoulder.

As usual, time cured most things, and Jackie settled down and became a very sweet baby boy, much to Little Spirit and John's relief.

John sometimes watched Little Spirit while he slept, or he snuck into the school and watched him interact with the students or faculty. He marveled at Little Spirit's ability to work with and handle people, but he was even more surprised by the fact that anyone that met Little Spirit felt a great love he shared so easily, and they quickly loved him back.

As Jackie grew, he became more and more independent but also more free-spirited and feisty. He tried ever so hard to keep up with his brothers and did pretty well. However, the only person who lit up his world every time was his daddy, Little Spirit. In that little boy's eyes, this man did no wrong. John agreed with him.

One early morning, Little Spirit and John were in the throes of lovemaking, and out of the darkness, they heard Jackie's voice. "You stop hurting Daddy! Dad, I'm telling on you. I'll tell Gwamma, and she'll be mad and get her spoon." John couldn't help but laugh out loud.

Little Spirit put him back to bed. When he returned and crawled back into bed, he showed John love without reason. John saw him later that day, and Little Spirit still glowed of romance. John nearly took him there in his office. However, Donna and John-Lee put a stop to that.

John-Lee, it turned out, thought he was the self-appointed chief of school security. Donna fumed with anger as it seemed that John-Lee had become quite the little boss. He used the fact his daddy, Little Spirit, was head of the school, and his dad, John Two Hawks, was a Chief and head of the reservation's security. He threw his weight around and bullied some of the students. John-Lee decided that Donna, *a mere woman*, needed to be put in her place. World War Three broke out. Donna informed Little Spirit and John about John-Lee's rude and bullying behavior.

John-Lee's inappropriate behavior really upset Little Spirit. Both he and Donna were visibly angry, their eyes fixed on John-Lee.

"Dr. Little Spirit, I'll handle this with my son."

"Our son." Little Spirit's face truly expressed his unhappiness.

"Sorry, our son. Come with me, boy. We need to have a father-to-son and chief-to-tribe member talk."

John-Lee's little feet only touched the ground a couple of times as John hauled him out of the school by his arm. He took him to the nearby prairie, and they sat and looked out at the horizon.

"Dad, are you mad at me?"

John didn't answer him. He just kept looking at the horizon. After a few more minutes, the herd of bison started to come over the horizon. They both saw that bison moved as a herd, the young protected by their mothers and the entire herd protected by the bulls.

Finally, John spoke, "John-Lee *Wá Wakíŋyaŋ*." He called

him his Lakota name, and that caught the boy's attention. John quietly told John-Lee about the herd's makeup, and John-Lee watched and listened to him. "The herd's like our tribe. Do you see how they all work as one to protect the young and the old? No one animal in the herd is boss."

"What about the bulls, Dad? They're bosses."

"That's very true, but they've earned the right to be chief. They've proven that they're strong and fearless and willing to fight to protect the herd. They'd even give up their lives to keep the rest of the herd safe. This didn't happen because of who their parents are, but because each earned that position."

A playful young calf bolted out of the herd off in a different direction, and just as suddenly, wolves appeared and chased after it, but its mother and several bulls chased it down and brought it quickly back to the herd.

"See what happens when a member of the herd doesn't follow the rules? The entire herd could be at risk. You, my son, are still only a member of our Lakota herd. You haven't earned the right to be a leader. You used your daddy's and my positions to bully your way around the other children and people. This isn't the Lakota way. You come from a powerful and dedicated family, but we don't threaten or bully our people. We guide and advise. And most importantly, we respect our elders. Do you understand me, John-Lee?" John saw big tears as they fell onto John-Lee's lap.

He nodded his little head. "I'm sorry, I was just trying so hard to be like you and Daddy. I guess I've some things I need to mend up, huh, Dad?"

"Yes, and you need to start with Auntie Donna, understood? Now get up and scoot back to school. You've some fixing to do."

"That's it? You aren't going spank me?" John-Lee's eyes were huge with anticipation.

"Nope, now scoot."

He flung himself into John's arms and hugged him tight, and off he ran as fast as his little legs could go back to school. John smiled as he watched the little guy.

John loved all three of their children. Little Spirit knew that discipline wasn't always his strong suit, but when push came to shove, he did the appropriate and loving thing. Chief John Two Hawks demonstrated outstanding leadership — he led by example and taught his children the same way, and most of the time, that worked.

John decided that John-Lee needed a bow and arrow set for his seventh birthday. Little Spirit argued totally against it as he felt John-Lee was too young to grasp the dangers of any misuse. John lectured Little Spirit on how he would train him to use the set appropriately. After all, the tips of all the arrows had rubber suction cups on them. He also reminded Little Spirit that many of the boys John-Lee's age owned a bow and arrow set already. Little Spirit knew that was true, so he relented.

One afternoon a few months later, John stormed into the house, boy in one hand, bow and arrows in the other. He fumed with anger. John's face turned scarlet red. John put their son on the couch and the bow and arrow on top of the refrigerator. He then returned to their son and spoke. Little Spirit could hear the controlled anger in his voice.

"John-Lee, you shot me on purpose, and it really hurt."

Little Spirit totally freaked. "You shot Dad with that weapon? John, how did this come about? After all, there are rubber suction cups on every arrow, and you were going to teach him, remember? He was going to be the expert bowman, right?"

John flushed and looked embarrassed. "Little Spirit, you

were right, and I was wrong. He's too young to understand how dangerous weapons can be. It seems your son removed the rubber tips, then used the pencil sharpener to hone them to a very sharp point."

John put his hand on his wounded butt and brought it back covered with blood. Little Spirit saw the blood that came from John's backside. He rushed off to retrieve the medical kit. "God, John, are you okay? Do I need to call an ambulance?"

John answered him, "It hurts like hell, but it didn't go in far. I'll be fine."

Seeing the blood, John-Lee squealed in fear. "Eye eee, I killed Dad!" John-Lee sobbed.

His dad picked him up and held him close. "I'm not killed yet, but almost."

Losing his precious bow and arrows was very hard on John-Lee, but he took his punishment without protest.

Later, John told Little Spirit what had transpired. He and John-Lee were out picking up trash and pulling weeds around the Council Hall. When John bent over to pick up a soda can, he felt the arrow pierce his behind. It seemed that John-Lee found his butt to be a perfect target, so he fired at it and made a direct hit.

John took a ton of teasing from his friends and family. John heard all the jokes. *Maybe he needed a new pair of butt skin boots,* or *it's a good thing you were facing away from that boy of yours, or he would've had weenie on a stick.* John took the ribbing in his normal stride. He laughed at everyone's jokes.

One night a couple of months away from the arrow incident, he and Little Spirit were cuddled up in bed.

"Little Spirit, you never teased me or joked about me being shot in the butt, nor did you even one time say I told you so. Why?"

"John, the thought of losing you is so incredibly

frightening to me that I saw no humor in it, nor did I think saying anything negative would help. John, you were shot. My life and love are in your hands. You're half of my soul, and living without you'd be impossible." Little Spirit snuggled in close and held on tight.

"You aren't going to let him have another set of bow and arrows, are you?"

"Oh, he can have another set," Little Spirit mumbled.

"Really!" John stared at him in shock.

"Yeah, when he's thirty."

"Now, that's the Little Spirit I know and love." John laughed and drew Little Spirit in closer. They didn't sleep much that night.

Summer came and turned warm. It was a time for some work but also time off to play. The family had planned a trip that summer to visit Grandpa and Grandma McIntire's farm.

Jackie fell deeply in love with Grandma McIntire and followed her everywhere, and she told everyone she felt over the moon about it. They cooked and baked and mixed and cleaned up to start over with the next meal. Jackie shined with pride over the delicious food they cooked. John and John-Lee helped Little Spirit's dad and brothers with chores. John-Lee worked alongside the men without a single complaint. He quickly pointed out things that he could do by himself, and Grandpa McIntire and John encouraged him to go for it.

John-Lee appeared from the barn frantic. "Grandpa, Dad, come quick, there's a cow having trouble calving!" He fled back into the barn with John and Andy right behind him.

"John-Lee, stay far back from that heifer. She could be dangerous if she's in pain and struggling!" Andy shouted, too late. They found John-Lee right next to the struggling heifer, and he touched her and softly spoke, which calmed her down, so she went with her contractions instead of fighting them.

Andy climbed into the pen to assist with the birth, but John-Lee said to him, "Don't pull yet. She isn't ready." He spoke something in Lakota to the heifer, and she pushed, then pushed again. "Okay, Grandpa, do it now. The calf's in the right position, and she's ready for it to be born!"

Andy pulled and out swooshed a perfectly solid black heifer calf. John-Lee hurried to clean its nose and mouth, and the two of them stepped back. The cow rose and started cleaning her baby just like she should do.

John-Lee rubbed her neck and said, "*Tókheškhe yaúŋ he? Ya waste wičhíŋčala.*"

Andy looked to John for interpretation. "He asked her how she was and told her she's a good girl and great mother."

The young cow reached back and licked John-Lee's face, and that made him giggle.

Andy looked at John and said, "It's true he'll be a great healer for your people someday."

Later, Andy told his family and Little Spirit all about the miracle he'd witnessed and that his grandson possessed a great gift.

Little Andrew made everything into a scientific discovery with anything unknown that he found on the farm or the difference between the things he saw here and at home. He either parked himself on the computer or researched in books to prove his findings, then shared them with everyone and anyone.

John laughed at supper one evening after a long day. "John-Lee will be our healer and warrior. He's already developed that work-with-your-hands mindset, and it makes him so happy just working, but he's also so into medical stuff, who knows about this little man will want to be."

Little Spirit chuckled and agreed. "He has so many of your best traits."

John smiled warmly at Little Spirit and continued. "Little Andrew will be our biologist or research scientist, as anything to do with discovering living things fascinates him, and then he researches it. That kid knows more about the prairie animals than I do." The family laughed.

"Now, little Jackie's something else, I don't think I told you, Little Spirit, but this morning he was in Melissa's room all dressed up like for a fancy ball." Little Spirit's eyes widened. "Yep, I saw him myself. Here, I took pictures." John turned on his camera and showed Jackie all decked out in Grandma's clothes, shoes, jewelry, and makeup. "Little Spirit, you're doing that thing you do with your mouth, that fish mouth thing. Stop it! It gives me the creeps." John continued, "I asked Jackie about this, and he said he was a Lakota warrior ready to defend his land, but not before he and Grandma made cookies." John's laugh, deep and rich, came. Finally, John said, "So Little Spirit, it looks like we may have a chef brewing amongst us."

Later that night, Little Spirit whispered in John's ear, "I always knew that all that makeup and jewelry you wore made you a closet drag queen." John stiffened, then grabbed Little Spirit, tickling him all over.

"You take that back." John didn't let up until Little Spirit relented and took it back.

Then they heard Melissa through the wall. "Could you two tone it down? We have children in the house."

John moaned in complete humiliation, and Little Spirit tried not to snicker, but not successfully. John figured if everyone already thought they were making love, they might as well be doing just that. It took only a second, and his Little Spirit responded. He could never turn down John. They fit perfectly together. Their lovemaking lasted most of the night. One body, one spirit, one soul, even though they kept silent.

The love they shared spread throughout the farm as the next morning, everyone seemed to have that glow about them. The visit turned out just incredible.

One morning a few days before they were to leave, Melissa announced that she planned to cut the boys' hair.

John stood up from the kitchen table. "You'll do no such thing. They're Lakota."

Andy looked sternly at his wife. "Are you clear on that matter?"

She blushed and said, "Perfectly."

Later that day, Little Spirit and John talked. "John, you handled that situation so beautifully. My mother can be a force to reckon with sometimes."

"Thank you, but if she'd cut their hair, she'd have cut us out of her life forever. I know she thought they would look cuter with short hair, but it isn't Lakota. Thank goodness she asked first. I'm sort of surprised she just didn't cut their hair and surprise us."

"Me, too."

Many tears flowed as Little Spirit and his family said their goodbyes. Departures brought some hurt and sadness. John knew that Little Spirit missed his parents, and it'd be a while before he'd see them again. The three boys had grown very attached to their grandparents, and it was hard for them to say goodbye, too.

Arriving back home brought happiness and a feeling of calm back. It was good to be home.

Chapter Eighteen

From their front porch, Little Spirit called and called John-Lee, but got no response. He phoned John, and he hadn't seen him since breakfast. "John, where can he be? After his last wandering off, you would think he would remember to tell us where he planned on going." Little John had worn him out the last time he wandered off on one of his adventures and was gone for six hours with no one knowing his whereabouts.

John got silent. "Can you hear that?"

"Hear what?"

"Just listen."

Little Spirit then heard the drums. "Drums, John, what does that mean?"

John quickly replied, "It's coming from the center. I'll meet you there."

Little Spirit hung up and said to Andy, "Watch Jackie, I'm going to the center."

"Are you kidding? We're going, too."

They took off, all three of them. Little Spirit hurried ahead and said, "Andy, you bring Jackie."

He and John arrived at the same time. As they rounded the building there John-Lee stood, pounding the drums as hard as he could. Beside him laid Tȟuŋkášila Waŋblí, Great-Grandfather. John rushed to Tȟuŋkášila Waŋblí and pulled him onto his lap. Little John-Lee still pounded the drums with all his might.

Little Spirit got to him and wrapped his arms around him,

which ceased the drums. "*No*, Daddy, if I stop, the spirits will take him." Tears flowed down his little cheeks.

Little Spirit looked to John. His face said it all as he shook his head and cried.

"John-Lee, you're so brave and did everything right, but son, it's his time to go be with the Great Father and to be with those who've gone before him."

"But, Daddy, I love him so much. Who'll teach me what he knows?"

"Everyone will," Little Spirit answered and pulled his sobbing son in close. As people arrived, they immediately joined John in the mourning chants.

Thomas Two Elks arrived and saw his beloved grandfather in John's arms. The sound he made stabbed through everyone's heart. "*Wakȟáŋ Tȟáŋka wičála wanáǧi tȟa- Tȟuŋkášila!*" He took Tȟuŋkášila Waŋblí from John and held him, then rocked back and forth. He sang the song to send the spirit of Tȟuŋkášila Waŋblí to the safety of the Holy Place. His pain and sorrow flowed through the air. Great sorrow came upon all that arrived.

The drums started again. John-Lee started it, and soon others joined on the other drums. Little John-Lee drummed until he exhausted himself. Finally John stepped in and picked up John-Lee, and Hank immediately took his place. John-Lee put his head on his father's shoulder and cried until exhaustion wore him out and he slept. The body of Tȟuŋkášila Waŋblí was taken to be prepared for his burial. John and Little Spirit left for home, and John carried a sleeping John-Lee.

Tȟuŋkášila Waŋblí's burial ceremony turned into a huge event. Within a couple of days, hundreds of people came from all over the country to send him off to the Sacred Land of the Great Father. People of all races stood side by side and said their prayers to send him to the Holy Place. Drums beating and chanting continued until they reached the burial site.

Chief Thomas Two Elks simply raised his hand, and all went instantly silent. "My grandfather, the Great Tȟuŋkášila Waŋblí, wrote this to be read now at this time." He paused only a second. He took a deep breath and read aloud.

"*Mitȟáwa wakȟáŋheža* . . . my children, it's my time to go to the Great Father and be with those that have gone before me. I've taught you what you need to know, and it's now your turn to teach others. We're Lakota, we're strong, and we're proud. Now, send me off to the Holy Land with celebration."

They buried Tȟuŋkášila Waŋblí in the sacred ground, and for three days, the chanting and drums continued. Suddenly they just stopped. John and Little Spirit's family were sitting at the breakfast table when all went silent.

John-Lee bowed his head and said, "Does that mean he crossed over safely, Dad?"

John quietly answered him, "Yes, he's with our family and friends that have been waiting for him on the other side. There'll be no tears now. We don't want to have him think we're too sad to be without him. We must celebrate his life as he's begun a new one in the Holy Land."

Little Spirit held back his tears for Tȟuŋkášila Waŋblí and said, "I'll miss that gentle, wise, old man so terribly much. Be with God."

The celebration began for the beautiful life of Tȟuŋkášila Waŋblí. No one would ever forget old Tȟuŋkášila Waŋblí. Little Spirit told Thomas, "I know he's smiling down on his people with pride."

Thomas smiled. "I know that, too."

Chapter Nineteen

Summer passed quickly, and school started back into session. Little Spirit was busy with all the duties necessary for running the school.

The day was a particularly beautiful fall day, and everyone enjoyed it. But uneasiness fell on some the people.

Hank commented to John, "Why are you so restless?"

As John sat with the Council of Chiefs, he told the council that something just felt wrong, terribly wrong, because his hawk was tearing him apart inside. He could feel its desperate need to protect. "It feels like my hawk's desperate to get free."

The school sirens suddenly blared. Next, the general alarms blasted. John jumped up and shouted, "There's trouble at the school!"

Every man bolted out the door, and they ran for the school. As John ran, dozens of other people joined him. Hank threw him a rifle, and they kept going. John heard shouting and multiple gunshots. He saw the children and teachers as they ran out the side doors of the school as fast as they could and into the surrounding prairie, where they lay flat. They disappeared into safety. It looked like most of the kids escaped unharmed. They heard several more shots, then silence. John's hawk screamed for all to hear as he charged the building, hellbent on stopping whatever rampage was happening. John's hawk knew what he would find, but his human part wouldn't allow it. He met several members of the tribe at the door. They carried guns, and John raised his rifle, but they were friends, not foes. They blocked the entrance door of the school.

John's one question, "Little Spirit? Is Little Spirit okay?"

"Chief John Two Hawks, I think it's best you stay outside and let security do its job. The sheriff's department is on the way. All of the attackers are dead or taken into our custody," Rendy Grey Wolf said, blocking him from entering.

"I am security! How many children were injured or lost?" John asked, his voice trembling.

"None, thanks to that Little Spirit of yours. John, he fought them off as long as he could, as did your sister, Donna Yellow Bird."

"How many of our staff have been injured or . . . killed" The painful truth hit him all of a sudden.

"John, we lost five staff members, and four more were injured. Please don't, stay here and let—" Rendy Grey Wolf's words came too late.

John pushed passed him and shoved open the doors to the school. There lay his sister, Donna, all bloody and shot up, and as he moved farther in, he saw him. His Little Spirit, he laid in a pool of blood that slowly flowed out of him.

"Nooooooo!" John screamed and threw himself on Little Spirit's shredded body. John frantically tried to push the blood back into his little body. His hawk screamed. John screamed, too.

He pulled his Little Spirit into his lap and held him, rocking him back and forth. John begged, willing him, "Breathe, please God, I beg you, don't take away the only person I'll ever love." John held his lifeless body as he pulled off his own shirt and used it to help stop the blood flow. John felt no life in Little Spirit's body. "Little Spirit, if you leave me now, I'll have nothing to live for. Little Spirit Jackson Lee McIntire Two Hawks, I can't exist without you."

Rendy tapped John's shoulder. "Look!"

There, Little Spirit had written in his own blood, *I love you, Joh*—the rest ended in a smear.

John looked at Rendy. "I swear to all that we hold holy that wasn't there when I got to him," John said, his voice full of emotion. John felt for a pulse on his wrist, arm, and neck, and he felt it, so faint, but present. John screamed, "Help me! My God, help me! He's alive! *YaŋkÁ kičhí miyé Tákula Wakȟáŋ*, stay with me, Little Spirit!"

Jena arrived at his side, and she concurred that she, too, felt a heartbeat, albeit very faint. She couldn't comprehend how. "There are so many holes in his body and blood everywhere, but there's a heartbeat."

The paramedics arrived and tried to take Little Spirit. John's voice roared, "No! If you take him from me, he'll die!"

Jena piped in, "I think he's right! I think him holding him somehow stopped the bleeding. Take them together, and carefully."

No one argued. They simply got them both into the ambulance, and they were off. Medics shouted orders and did what they could in the ambulance. They had to start an IV, but neither was having any luck due to the significant blood loss. As a last resort, they put it in Little Spirit's neck, and it worked.

That ride from the reservation to the hospital was frightening at times. It was as if Little Spirit would leave them, but then his heart would beat again. John heard them say they might not save him if they didn't move it. The anguish on his face told it all.

John pleaded, "Guys, you need to step on it. He's fading. I can feel it." The ambulance lurched forward as the driver hit the gas.

More than twenty people waited at the emergency room doors, ready to help as soon as the ambulance pulled up. The medic explained the situation carefully, and the attending physicians seemed to understand immediately. Dr. Howard Taft spoke to John, "You know me, and I know you. You're going to have to trust me. We're going to have to extract

Jackson from you. We'll be careful, but we need to get Jackson to surgery ASAP!"

"He's Little Spirit," John said as he kissed his lover's head.

Dr. Taft nodded. "Okay, Little Spirit, then. We need to get him to the O.R. Now! John, do you understand what I'm saying? We need to do it now, or he'll surely die."

"Take him."

Quickly, personnel took Little Spirit from John's embrace and immediately applied pressure to his wounds.

Dr. Taft saw the panic and fear on John's face. "I'll do my very best for your Little Spirit, I promise." They instantly disappeared.

John stood there, his clothes covered in blood—Little Spirit's blood. He didn't know what to do. Suddenly, his whole world crashed in around him. He leaned against the wall, covered his face, and cried and prayed and cried some more. Staff turned away or bowed their heads as he let his sorrow pour out.

John gathered his inner strength and pulled himself together, and said aloud, "I've got to stay strong for Little Spirit." He straightened up and saw the medics from the ambulance. John thanked them for all their help.

"My name's Ron. I'm the chief medic in the ambulance service. Man, I'm going to find you some scrubs to wear and a place you can shower, okay?"

John shook his head. "No, I'm staying here until I know what's happened to my husband."

The guy shook his hand and left.

An hour later, John's mother and father arrived, as did Hank and Screaming Eagle. Jena hugged him, as did his father.

Screaming Eagle looked at John. "Man, you need to clean up. Let me find out how and where you can do that."

"No! I won't leave this spot until they tell me about my Little Spirit." Tears rolled down John's cheeks.

Screaming Eagle nodded and sat.

Hank asked, "Have you heard anything?"

John shook his head no.

Hank then asked, "How are you holding up?"

John shook his head and said, "I can feel him fading away, and I'll go with him if he has to go to the Holy Place."

Jena got up into John's face. "You'll never say . . . or even think something like that ever again. Who do you think will raise those three beautiful sons, answer me that!"

"God, Ma. Are the boys okay?" John said, and again, the tears began to roll. She pulled him down into a hug.

"They are fine, son. I promise they are."

The minutes ticked by slowly. Three hours and forty-five minutes passed from the time they took Little Spirit to surgery, and finally, the doctor emerged from behind the O.R. doors. He looked immensely sad and tired.

"John, that Little Spirit of yours is something else. How he survived, first being shot five times, then in an ambulance all the way here, plus almost four hours of surgery, I'll never understand. I can't tell you how many units of blood we've given that little guy. But, John, somehow, he made it through. I'll never be able to explain how or why, yet he did."

John collapsed to his knees, sat back, pulled himself into a ball, and sobbed.

"Son, you stand up and thank the Great One. Your man's still alive." Thomas helped him rise.

The doctor spoke again, "John, you've got to listen to me, and carefully. Little Spirit isn't nearly out of the woods. He's super-critical, and even if we get past this, in all probability, there may be brain damage due to lack of blood. John, he's on total life support."

John looked him straight in the eyes. "When can I see him? I need to be close so he can draw strength from me."

Dr. Taft hesitated. "First, you're going to clean up, and I'll arrange that. You can't go into ICU with all that dried blood and all that bacteria you're carrying. You can see him in fifteen minutes, if you're ready."

The doctor left, and within a couple of minutes, a nurse arrived with some blue scrubs. "Mr. Two Hawks, follow me, please," she said.

John looked at his family and asked Screaming Eagle, "Will you come with me? Hank, please, will you stay with my folks?" John got to the room where he could shower and change clothes. He quickly stripped and showered.

Screaming Eagle handed John a towel and the scrubs. "Who all did we lose?" John asked quietly.

Ever so solemnly, Screaming Eagle answered, "Your sister, Donna Yellow Bird."

John had seen her—he already knew, but he still gasped.

"Robert Red Fox, Helen Gordon, and Mike Turtle, and there were four more injured, none seriously. No children were even scratched, thanks to your sister and Little Spirit and the others."

John and Screaming Eagle returned to find John's parents sobbing. Panic set in.

However, Hank saw his face and intervened. "The loss of Donna just really hit home, and they're taking it pretty hard."

John walked over and hugged them both.

Dr. Taft suddenly charged into the room. "John, you need to come quick. There may not be much time left. Little Spirit's struggling."

The two of them flew down the hall to the ICU and into Little Spirit's room. They entered the room, where every light was flashing and alarms beeped. The little man was struggling to stay alive.

John raced to Little Spirit's side and took his hand. "*Čhaŋtóčhignake*, I love you so much, Little Spirit. We're one in mind, body, and spirit. Live for me, live for us, please." Slowly, one by one, the flashing lights ceased, and the alarms quieted. John gave Dr. Taft a frightened look.

"No, John, this is good. It means his body functions are more near normal. He isn't crashing anymore."

John looked at Little Spirit. "Honey, you don't have to cause such a ruckus. I'm not ever going anywhere. I'll always be here. Can you hear me? I'm never going anywhere."

Dr. Taft looked over Little Spirit and all of the machines that monitored him. "We were lucky this time, John," Dr. Taft said.

"Well, Doc, you best make arrangements for me to stay, or it'll happen again. I promise to do as I'm told. Just don't let them kick me out."

Clearly fighting back his own emotions, Dr. Taft cleared his throat and said, "Consider it done."

Several times, John's Little Spirit started to crash in the first twenty-four hours. He got so many units of blood it worried John that they might run out. The ICU nurse told John, "Nearly two hundred people from the reservation already donated blood, and they said there'd be more tomorrow. Little Spirit's blood typed B-positive, but we used all of what we had here, so we started to give him O-negative or positive. They are the best substitute."

At ten AM, just twenty-five hours from the surgery, John heard Melissa McIntire's voice. "Lady, I don't care who you are, get the hell out of my way. I'm going to see my baby boy." She entered the room with fear plastered on her face. The nurses quickly gowned, masked, and gloved her. She saw that her Jackson was barely alive. "What can we do?" her brokenhearted voice asked.

John quickly responded, "Do any of the ones that came with you have B-positive blood?" Melissa quickly gathered her wits and raced out of the room in a shot. She returned back within minutes.

As the nurse re-prepped her, she said, "John, there are eight of us here, and I sent them to the blood bank to donate. Most of the McIntire's have B-positive blood. Now, my beautiful son-in-law, it's time for you to go home and get cleaned up. I'll stay with Jackson."

John looked at Melissa like she had three heads. "I'll not leaving Little Spirit until he knows I'm here. Melissa, he stops doing well when I go too far away, even for a few minutes. I won't leave my Little Spirit until he knows if he's going to stay with us."

Tears rolled down her cheeks, but she nodded her understanding.

"Little Spirit, it seems that a big part of your McIntire clan's here. They all need to see you." He kissed Little Spirit's hand, but there wasn't any response or sign of him waking. John looked at the clock on the wall. It was twenty-seven hours since Dr. Taft had finished the surgery. One milestone hurdled.

Later that afternoon, Little Spirit started to slip away again. Dr. Taft decided that he must have been still bleeding internally and that he needed to operate one more time to find it. John and the doctor went into the waiting room, and all the families gathered around them.

Dr. Taft explained, "Little Spirit's going to need more surgery. It's his only chance to survive. He's been prepped, and they're waiting for me now."

Andy McIntire looked angry and said to the doctor, "How can this be?"

"Your son came to me with five bullets in him that bounced around in his tiny torso. When I opened him up, his upper left lung lobe was destroyed, his stomach looked like it went through a paper shredder, and he had a nick on his aorta. His right kidney was severely damaged, and he had tears in his intestines. I repaired everything I could, but with the amount of blood and damage, something got missed, and I intend to find it."

The doctor turned and left.

Andy spoke softly, "I'm sorry, John, I lost my head, and my big mouth just fired off."

All stood silent. Then John heard it first, the sound of singing. The voice sounded so beautiful, full of hope and joy. One by one, all the others heard it, too. Melissa asked, "It's so beautiful. What's the song?"

John responded, "It's the Lakota song of life."

Everyone listened, and they waited.

Time moved by so slowly. Hours came and went, and John paced and watched for the door to open. Every hour, a little nurse came by to give John and the families an update. Every time she entered the room, everyone jumped up. Nothing sounded very hopeful or good. "He's still in surgery and is hanging in there," or, "We had to give him five more units of blood."

"I'm about to lose my mind," John mumbled, but he held it together. Every minute got longer and longer. his family encouraged him to hang in there, and he pushed himself through as every hour passed. He asked his mother how the kids were doing. She told him they were struggling with what was happening, but his family was taking care of them.

Finally, three hours after he'd started, Dr. Taft flew into the waiting room. "John, I need you to come with me right now!"

John panicked, but before fear engulfed him, he followed

him.

"I think we got him fixed up, but he isn't responding well. I need you to work your soul mate magic one more time."

John only nodded, but he was terrified that he might lose Little Spirit. They reached the O.R., and there was blood everywhere. Little Spirit was hooked up to all kinds of machines, and tubes seemed to run from all over his body. John gasped because it all looked so threatening. Little Spirit looked so frail and delicate.

Dr. Taft tapped him on his shoulder. "You need to mask, gown, and glove up, right now. He won't make it unless he has a reason to fight. John, his heartbeat's weaker than it should be, and his blood pressure's so incredibly low we can't get a reading. How he's alive, I'm not sure."

John's warrior came to life. He reached around the tubing and machines and embraced his Little Spirit's hand. "You listen to me! I'm here, your families are here, and they're all rooting for you. Are you listening to me? I can't live if you're not here with me. Little Spirit! Fight for me! Fight for our beautiful children! Please live!"

Dr. Taft's eyes widened. Then he whispered, "My God! It's working."

Little Spirit's heart rate increased, not to the level it needed to be, but it had risen to a more rapid pace. His blood pressure went from the machine being unable to get anything to a low reading, not great, but an improvement.

"Little Spirit, come back to me, please," John bent and kissed his forehead.

Dr. Taft had brought back the nursing staff and orderlies. "Please prep our patient to be moved to the ICU."

John kissed his Little Spirit's head.

Then Dr. Taft said, "Let's get him rolling. Moving may be hard on Little Spirit, so we need to do it as quickly as possible. The room in ICU is ready and waiting for his arrival." The move went swiftly, with no stops or slowdowns. A nurse ran ahead of them and shouted for everyone to clear out of the way. The forceful, loud woman made everyone in the way scatter like rats. The move proved hard on Little Spirit, his heart rate went down, and his blood pressure dropped, too. However, as soon as John slid beside him and took his hand, Little Spirit improved.

"Wait," John told them, then turned to Dr. Taft. "You've been my miracle worker. Thank you. Let his parents and my parents come in and see him alive. You don't know if he'll be here much longer, and their love and prayers will only help. Please."

The doctor left like a shot. Within minutes, John could hear footsteps running down the corridor toward them.

Melissa McIntire entered first, gowned, gloved, and masked. She didn't hesitate. She came there to see her son, and nothing else mattered to her. She took Little Spirit's hand and kissed it.

Jena walked to the foot of the bed. Tears of joy, fear, and pain flowed. She raised her eyes to the heavens and raised her hands to the sky, and with such raw emotion, she chanted, *"Ate Wakantanka, Lé mičhíŋča yeló, čha tȟaŋháŋ Tȟáwa Makȟá wičhóni takómni táku kiŋ iyúha ki Uŋkítȟawapi thiyóšpaye. Ičhé iyówiŋkhiyA uŋkíye úŋ Tákula Wakȟáŋ. Philámayaye, Wakantanka."*

Melissa looked at John.

He translated. "Father, Great Spirit, take care of my son. His life on earth means everything to his entire extended family. Please allow us to keep Little Spirit. Thank you, Great Spirit." Tears rolled down every cheek in that room.

Melissa said a solid, "Amen."

"Amen." Thomas and Andrew stood in the doorway.

Dr. Taft said to John and Little Spirit's parents, "I knew that willing someone to live and loving them enough to make it all happen was possible, but I'm seeing it for the first time in my life with my own eyes."

Jena tilted her head toward the doctor. "It's a Native American Spiritual bond, and it lasts forever." She smiled at Thomas Three Elks, took his arm, and patted Melissa's back. They headed for the waiting room to tell all who sat in the waited that they'd made it over another hurdle.

Little Spirit still lived.

John stayed at Little Spirit's side night and day. He seldom slept and ate next to nothing. He bathed Little Spirit, helped prop him so he wouldn't get bed sores, and he talked to him. He listened and watched for him to be Little Spirit. People tried over and over to get him to leave and get something to eat and some rest, but John Two Hawks refused to leave. Even as much as a force his mother, Jena, tried to be, she never budged him from Little Spirit's side. "Ma, I'll never forgive myself if something happened to him while I was taking care of me instead of him."

Four days passed by since the last surgery on Little Spirit, and it seemed to almost everyone that little change had occurred, but John and Dr. Taft knew that Little Spirit was growing stronger.

On day five, Dr. Taft decided to remove the breathing tube and take Little Spirit off the ventilator. John protested, but Melissa and Jena agreed with Dr. Taft and held their ground.

"John, he hasn't used the ventilator for nearly twelve hours. It's time," Dr. Taft told him. John finally caved, and they removed the tube. Little Spirit breathed on his own accord. Everyone held their collective breathes, but he continued breathing and even got stronger.

That night, Dr. Taft felt that Little Spirit had grown strong enough for John to go home and clean up and get something to eat, then get some much-needed rest. John refused to leave.

Later that night, Little Spirit moved his mouth like he

needed a drink. John called in the nurse, and she gave him some ice chips. Little Spirit swallowed. John danced around in a tiny circle with excitement. The nurse told him that they were slowly withdrawing the medication that put him in an induced coma.

A couple of hours later, Screaming Eagle and Hank came to check on John and Little Spirit. They tried to convince him that he needed to get food and clean up.

Dr. Taft arrived to check on his patient.

They heard a deep raspy voice say, "John." He looked at Dr. Taft, Screaming Eagle, and Hank, but none had spoken.

"John Two Hawks."

He heard his name again. He turned and said to Little Spirit, "Did you call for me?"

"John, you need to go," Little Spirit spoke. His voice was weak, but clear.

John's spirit soared. "You talked to me!" John's tears started to flow, and he couldn't stop them. "I'm never leaving you."

Little Spirit's weak, raspy voice stated, "No, you neeeed a shower. You stink. As for the rest of you, hush."

His Little Spirit came back. John knew it because Little Spirit always woke up very grumpy.

John looked at Hank and Screaming Eagle with that questioning look. "Did you hear him? He talked. My God, he talked. That means he's going to be all right, doesn't it, Doc? I got to go tell Ma and Dad and Melissa and Andy and everyone!" John's spirit floated on air.

"John," Little Spirit whispered. John instantly returned and took his hand.

"Yes, Little Spirit?"

"Don't come back until you've showered. What're all these people doing in my bedroom? Get them out. Don't be too long. I love you. Where am I?"

John started to explain everything to Little Spirit, but the doctor stopped him. "Not yet, John. He's still in a dream state of half awake and half asleep. All that stuff will come later."

John kissed Little Spirit's hand and forehead then told him he loved him and hurried out of the room to spread the good news to the family.

Then while John was still standing in the waiting room, Screaming Eagle, Hank, and Thomas took this opportunity to grab him and haul him out to the parking lot. "You're going home and getting cleaned up. You're going to eat and then rest for at least two hours. Do you read me?" Chief Thomas Three Elks directed so assertively that John only nodded. "Now, climb into the back of the pickup. You stink too bad to ride inside the truck. Your mother and Little Spirit's mother have things under control here. Now move it." Again, Thomas meant just what he said.

John sniffed himself and said to Hank and Screaming Eagle, "Come on, I can't smell that terrible." The deadpan looks told him differently.

They took him home for a shower, some food, and rest.

Just as he finished eating, his father joined him. "Now, John, before you go off half-cocked, you need to listen to me carefully. Two days ago, your son, little John-Lee, came to us, sobbing. When your mother and I finally got him settled down, he told us that we needed to find him a new home as you wouldn't love him anymore."

John was confused and he rose and started to quickly look around for his son. Thomas continued, "John, sit down, for God's sake, and listen! He was in the office the day of the attack, being scolded by Little Spirit because he kissed a little girl on the playground and made her cry. That was when the men burst into the building. Little Spirit charged up and took out the first one and then the second of the eight men. All of this was witnessed by John-Lee.

"It was the leader of the group, some crazy minister, that shot his daddy, but Little Spirit had more than just his school to protect. His son was in the line of fire. He screamed for John-Lee to run and find his dad and his Uncle Hank. He took off but remembered to hit the emergency alert before he got too far, and now the little guy blames himself for his daddy being shot, and he believes Little Spirit's going to die because he didn't stay and fight to protect him.

"John, I know you need to get to him but let me finish. It was about then that Donna came out with her bat swinging. She got two more before they took her out, and Little Spirit took the last bullets from the minister's gun. The other teachers and staff joined in to stop them, and even though we lost several more of our people, they were able to overtake those horrid animals. Even the wounded helped finally take them down. It's about then you came in and found our Little Spirit. He thinks you hate him for not protecting the family and running off."

"Oh, God, no, I need to find him now, Dad, help me. Oh God, I can't get my breath. He's got to know that I'm so proud of him. He saved so many lives by setting off that alarm."

John's dad nodded and indicated for him to look behind him.

John turned and saw John-Lee. He stood there all alone in the world. John wiped his eyes, so his tears wouldn't show. There stood his boy, with his mouth open, his nose running and spit falling from his mouth, sobbing uncontrollably.

John approached him and spoke softly as not to spook him. "John-Lee, it's Dad. Son, I love you so much, and I'm so proud you did exactly what Daddy told you to do. It proves to me you're a fearless warrior, and because you listened, many, many lives were saved."

John-Lee looked directly into his eyes, as if he needed to

see that John spoke only the truth. John knew that this moment would either make or break his baby boy.

"Dad, I want Daddy back and not hurt." He sobbed out and ran to John, then flung himself into John's arms.

"Me, too, baby boy, me, too. But you'll always be mine and Daddy's son, and both of us are so proud of you. Do you understand me? You're my son forever and ever and ever! And Daddy's getting better." John held him so tight, and the two of them cried. "We have to keep praying that Daddy will keep getting better. Okay?" John-Lee nodded his head on John's shoulder.

John held on tight until John-Lee pushed away to be set down. The little guy smiled at John and Thomas. "I'm going to go help Screaming Eagle." He left. John and his father just stared at each other in confusion.

John played with and spoke with his children. He explained their daddy's condition. They all hugged and held onto each other.

Exhaustion finally wore him out, and he let Thomas and Kitten take the children outside so he could nap. Sleep came easily and quickly.

John awoke to Thomas' shouting, "John, something's happening at the hospital. You need to go immediately!" He sprang to his feet and had his shoes on and was out the door in seconds.

Jena met him at the door to Little Spirit's room. "John, he's alive." Those were the only words John needed to hear, and now he could calm down.

Dr. Taft joined them and told him that Little Spirit gradually woke up a little more and a little more as the day progressed, but as he became more awake, he became more agitated and combative. The staff restrained him as he fought as though fighting for his life. They needed him calm so he wouldn't damage his injuries.

Dr. Taft said to John, "I'm afraid to sedate him because he's on pain medications. I'm a bit afraid he would revert back to a comatose state. Work your magic, John."

John entered the room. "Little Spirit, are you giving these people a hard time?" Little Spirit's head was turned away but turned toward John as he spoke.

"Where've you been?"

"Do you know me?" John asked.

"I thought you were dead," Little Spirit said.

"Really, who do you think I am?" John asked.

"Have you been drinking? You're my husband and the father to my boys, Chief John Two Hawks. Why'd you leave me here to die all alone?" Little Spirit suddenly had a very wild look in his eye, like he could stare through John, "There're crazy people here in my school. They want my kids. John! They can't have them! Please protect my children!"

John quickly moved over to the side of the bed. He spoke gently as he untied Little Spirit's hands, then wrapped his arms around him as best he could. "Little Spirit, those men are all gone. You saved the kids, and now you're in the hospital recovering from multiple gunshot wounds and two major surgeries." John leaned over and kissed him. "You're my hero."

Little Spirit stirred. "No wonder I feel like shit. I need to get up and go to school. Are the children all okay? Where's everyone? What about everyone else?" John just nodded, smiled, and stroked Little Spirit's hair as he gently drifted off. The pain medication was taking effect, and he quieted.

Jena, Melissa, Dr. Taft, and two nurses stood at the doorway. Dr. Taft finally spoke, "How in the hell did you do that? He was like a wild tiger not two minutes ago. He didn't even know his own mother."

John replied, "He was back fighting off the attackers of his school. He'll know you now, but we need to be prepared for more PTSD episodes."

"John," Little Spirit said.

"I'm right here,"

"Am I going to live?"

"Yes, you are."

"Good, because I love you like crazy. Now, be quiet so Mom, Jena, and I can sleep. Thanks."

He gently dozed off again. Melissa covered her face and allowed her emotions to come through for the first time. Jena reached for her and the two held each other close.

The next couple of days were on again and off again with Little Spirit's behavior. Sometimes he appeared totally lucid, but then the next moment, he seemed lost and frightened and in battle with his attackers. When those episodes happened, he wouldn't know anyone but John, who'd always get him calmed down. All of that proved rough on Little Spirit's parents and family.

Jena told everyone, "Have patience and understanding. He went through hell, but he came back to us."

Teary-eyed, Melissa looked at Jena, then at everyone else. "But will he be my loving, sweet boy just like before?"

Suddenly, Little Spirit spoke, "Mom, you all need to stop talking about me like I'm not here. Oh my God, I just remembered John-Lee. He was there. Is he safe?"

John immediately reached for his hand, and soothingly he talked to him and stroked his hair. "John-Lee's perfect. He's a hero, since he was the one that pulled the alarm."

Little Spirit smiled through his tears. "That's such a relief. My brave little boy did that?" The expression on Little Spirit's face suddenly went dark. "Is everyone that was there that day safe?"

John calmly and thoughtfully replied, "Mainly because of

you, Donna, Robert Red Fox, Helen Gordon, and Mike Turtle, the children of our school escaped without even so much as a scratch, and the attackers were taken out. Some of those crazies died, and the few that didn't will rot in prison. They were a group of fanatics that believed they should take the children and teach them about God."

Little Spirit lay there quietly, absorbing what John had told him. All eyes fixed on him and waited to see if he fully understood the enormity of what transpired. "Where's Donna? Where are Robert, Helen, and Mike? Are they here in this hospital?" He looked at John, at his mother, then Dr. Taft, and finally, Jena. His expression changed to anguish—he knew. Little Spirit grabbed John's hand and pulled him in close enough to hug his neck. "Oh my God, No!" He sobbed. The sounds of pain Little Spirit made came from a heart that was pierced with sorrow. So much sorrow filled that room. Finally, they got to mourn the loss of their loved ones.

Later that night, Little Spirit had a perplexed look on his face.

The look got John's attention. "Little Spirit, why the look? What's bothering you?"

"John . . . I have this song in my head, and I think I've heard it a lot. The voice singing was so incredibly beautiful that I couldn't leave here because it called me to stay with you. I know it's crazy, but I can still hear her singing in my head." Little Spirit sang the song, and John cried and pulled him in close.

After a few moments, John explained, "That really did happen, and it's an old Lakota song that's sung to give life."

"Who was singing it?" Little Spirit asked.

"I've absolutely no idea."

Two days later, they moved Little Spirit out of ICU and into a regular room. That was the first step toward total recovery. Although still attached tubes and hooked up to an EKG machine, every day Little Spirit got so much stronger. John finally got to bring the children to see their daddy. Little Spirit still experienced on-again-off-again memory issues about the children. Sometimes, he recalled them, and sometimes they seemed not to be part of his memories. It worried him, and he told John and their parents about it.

Jena told Little Spirit, "It's normal, and it'll all work itself out."

The worry on his face faded away when John walked into the room. He carried Jackson and held Andy's hand, with John-Lee holding onto John's shirt.

Finally, reaching his arms out, Jackson smiled and shouted, "Daddy!" John put Jackson on the bed with Little Spirit. "Oh Daddy, oh Daddy, where've you been? I missed you. Are those booboos hurty? What's this? When you get to come home? I need you at home."

Andrew climbed gently onto the other side of the bed and hugged his daddy. "I missed you."

Little Spirit kissed them both. "I'm much, much, much better. I'll come home when the doctor takes out the tubes, which will be soon." Then he noticed John-Lee standing back close to the door. "Hi, John-Lee, I missed you so much. Come here so I can get a big hug from my hero."

John-Lee stood there for a moment and stared at Little Spirit. Then everything burst out of him. "You're hurt because I didn't help you. I ran, and I should've fought to keep you safe. That's what a warrior's supposed to do. I'm sorry, Daddy. I shoulda helped you."

"John, bring him to me."

John brought him and picked up Jackson so John-Lee could be closer to his daddy. Little Spirit took both of John-Lee's hands, and with love that radiated throughout the room, he told John-Lee, "Look at me. You saved my life and the lives of all the children in the school. You're my hero and the bravest Lakota warrior I've ever known. You followed my instructions exactly, and that makes you so brave and such a great warrior."

John-Lee let loose his emotions, and Little Spirit held him.

Finally, he looked directly at his daddy. "Really? You aren't ashamed to have me as your son?"

"No matter what, you're my son, and I love you. Whether you're a hero or not, I'd feel the same, and so does Dad. But you need to trust me. You're a hero."

Little Spirit was determined to go home and pushed hard for that to happen, and three days after the doctor removed the tubes, he got what he hoped. Little Spirit went home.

He never realized what the impact of seeing the school might cause until they drove near it. The second it came into view, Little Spirit went into a fight or flight mode. John pulled the car over and talked him down, and reassured him, "Honey, it's all over, and everyone's safe."

Chapter Twenty

It took another month until Little Spirit regained enough of his strength to go out of the house. At times he got frightened and depressed, and other times he was back to his old self.

He and John were sitting at the breakfast table. Little Spirit shuffled his food around and noticed John watching him.

John finally asked, "What's got you so deep in thought?"

Little Spirit looked up from his plate, feeling complete anguish. "I want to know why."

John tilted his head. "Why what?"

He quietly answered, "Why our little school? What could we have that they needed so much they'd kill for it?"

"They all belonged to this crazy religious cult. They came for the children to save them from paganism and debauchery. Honey, they were all insane crazies. The news reporters have been investigating the whole group. There are news reports all over the stations about their cult. They were filled with so much hatred and insaneness."

Little Spirit scowled at John and said, "For what they did to the people I love, I hope they burn in hell."

John took his hand and squeezed it. "Me, too."

Little Spirit walked inside his school for the first time since the attack. He had John at his side and held John's hand tightly, afraid to let go. For a brief second, the whole horrible episode replayed in his mind. When it stopped, Little Spirit took a deep breath and pushed forward. He found the office empty and called Donna's name. Then he remembered she wouldn't answer him ever again. He turned to John. "It still hurts my soul. I loved her so much." He laid his head on John's chest and cried.

Then the drums started. "We've to go to the gym. The children planned something special. They needed to do this for you and for themselves. This whole ordeal was pretty hard on them, too. Some of them still struggle. I think seeing you back in this building will help."

Little Spirit grabbed John's arm and hugged it close, and as they walked down the corridor, the drums got louder. John pulled open the double doors to the gym, and they saw the huge crowd gathered there. Every person from the entire reservation attended. The children all sat in large circles, and everyone wore their finest ceremonial dress. Some of the children had painted their faces.

Little Spirit froze and just stood there. John took his hand and led him up to the middle circle. There stood all the chiefs of the nation, Jena, Little Spirit's parents and siblings, and his children.

"John, what's happening here?" Little Spirit asked, his voice quaked with emotion.

Chief Thomas Three Elks spoke, "We're here to celebrate life. Yours, Little Spirit, for which we're so very grateful that the Great Spirit let you stay with us, but also to celebrate the lives of those who aren't with us and have moved on to the Great Prairies beyond, the Holy Place."

Thomas stretched out his arm, indicating for Little Spirit to turn around. There on the wall behind him, he saw the huge murals of those that died saving the children of this school.

Little Spirit let out all of the emotions that'd been bottled up in him for months. His cry of anguish sounded more like an injured animal than human — the sound slowly turned into sobs. The silence of every person in that room showed they felt that pain, too.

John reached for him, but Little Spirit shook his head no.

He gathered himself and stood tall. Little Spirit walked toward the paintings, and the crowd made a path for him.

First, he reached his much-loved Donna's painting. It was a perfect likeness of her, and in the background stood her children and her loving Sally Anne. Little Spirit leaned against it and cried. Then he stepped back, kissed her hand, and touched Donna's face. Sally Anne stood there with her girls. Little Spirit pulled them all into a huge embrace. In the background, the sounds of muffled sobs could be heard.

Next came Robert Red Fox's painting. He looked so brave and tall, and the faces of his family surrounded him. Little Spirit put his hand on Robert's heart and quietly said, "Thank you for the great sacrifice you gave our children." His wife clutched her children and softly cried. He reached out and hugged Robert's family.

Then Little Spirit moved to Helen Gordon's painting. Although he didn't touch it, he said to her, "You were a great teacher and a strong woman. Thank you for being there for the children." He turned, and there stood Helen's mother. She reached her arms out to him, and Little Spirit stepped into them and embraced her.

Mike Turtle came last. His great love, Mina White Clover, stood close by, tears rolling down her sad face. She looked broken. Little Spirit paid his respects to Mike and thanked him for loving the children, then went to Mina, wrapped himself around her, and held her as they both mourned.

Suddenly someone started singing. It was the same song and voice he'd heard, that had kept him from going to the Great Father. He turned to see Sally Anne singing as she clung to her daughters. Little Spirit moved to her and engulfed her in his arms.

"You saved my soul, Sally Anne. Thank you." The little

girls joined the hug and smiled at their mother and uncle-father.

Chief Thomas interrupted, "Mourning time's now past. Now we'll celebrate their lives and that fact that we've our Little Spirit back."

The celebration began when John and Little Spirit's three sons brought Little Spirit bouquets of wildflowers. John whispered, "They've been out picking them all morning." Little Spirit took the flowers and bent down to kiss his sons, but John stopped him. "No, they're warriors respecting another warrior, no kissing." John smiled with pride at his family.

The drums and music started, and the three little guys began dancing. John-Lee and Andy moved carefully, following the traditional dance of celebration. Little Jackson, on the other hand, looked like he was at a disco. Little Spirit covered his mouth so as not to laugh out loud. The rest of the tribe joined the boys, and the celebration lasted for hours. People danced, talked, and laughed. It truly became a celebration of life.

After a couple of hours of celebration, Little Spirit's exhaustion began to show. He wanted to stay longer. John wanted none of that, and despite Little Spirit's loud protests, John took him home and put him to bed. They lay in bed and talked for a while.

Then Little Spirit looked deep into John's gaze and said, "I need you, John Two Hawks."

"You have me, Little Spirit Jackson Lee McIntire Two Hawks," John said and pushed Little Spirit's curly hair out of his face and looked directly into his loving eyes. He suddenly understood Little Spirit. John saw the man's smoldering passion.

They both desperately needed each other. John couldn't get

enough of this man he loved so much, and he made Little Spirit feel whole again.

About the Author

I am a retired educator living on a farm in the northeast Georgia Mountains. I spend time writing and tending the many animals on the farm. I live with my teenage son and my elderly father.